Mabel's Way

Other books by

Lila Hopkins

Christian Romantic Suspense

The Master Craftsman

Strike a Golden Chord

Weave Me a Song

Juvenile Novels

Talking Turkey

Eating Crow

To Mom, Grandma,
and Great Grandma.
Hope you enjoy this!
We love you!

Mabel's Way

Suspense, love and laughter at Dogwood Glenn

A NOVEL BY

Lila Hopkins

Lila Hopkins

Laurel Hills Books
www.lilahopkins.com
rhopkins27@nc.rr.com

Cover painting by Lila Hopkins
Book design by Luci Mott

ISBN-13: 978-1470153557
ISBN-10: 1470153556

Author's note

As I was writing this book, every neighbor and friend asked if they were going to be in it. "Yes, of course, but not so you will recognize yourself." My characters are composites of many people, with the exception of Mabel. Any good quality in her character is based on my friend, Mabel who lived across the hall from us. Any silly characteristic is based on me.

I stepped in to the pool one day and met a little black snake face to face. The first week we were here there was a tornado watch and we had to go to the first floor, much as I describe in the book. The scene in which Dev tells the dining room residents that a robber is on the loose is factual. I just took it a bit further.

I could not have thought up all the activities myself so much of the book is based on fact. I fell and broke my wrist once. I know what that means.

I wondered if the robbery scene would be plausible, but as I was working on the book, my husband was robbed ten feet from our building, by a knife-armed man.

Just remember that the book is fiction and enjoy it!

THIS BOOK IS LOVINGLY DEDICATED
TO THE MEMORY OF

Mabel Council Johnson

Close friend and neighbor

Acknowledgments

This would never have been written without
The persistent and unrelenting
"Good humor" nagging
Of the man across the hall:
Dr. Robert Holt

I am also indebted to these special friends:
Dr. Hampton Casebolt
Carol Flack
Fred Eargle
Richard Hopkins
Denise Owens
Trey Stanley
Rebecca Wilson
Beverle Weller

And always, my beloved editor:
Judith Geary

Mabel's Way

Chapter One

Mabel Peterman Yancey, on her early morning walk around the Dogwood Glenn Retirement Center, observed a young man, carrying garden shears, coming from the rear of the Wellness Center. She felt a strange disquietude. She hadn't seen him on the property before, but there was a vague familiarity about him. *Must be the new help for the gardener.*

"Don't murder the Crepe Myrtles," she called cheerfully.

He pulled his red cap down to shade his eyes, and fled down the street to where Manuel was pushing a wheelbarrow full of yellow and purple pansies.

"Well!" Mabel exclaimed. She was not used to being ignored, especially at a place where friendliness prevailed, always.

It was then that she heard the scream—a bloodcurdling wail. She nearly dropped her cane. The piercing screech came from the swimming pool in the Wellness Center. *Oh, my! Sounds like Ruthie Sue. I was to meet her there.*

She hurried to the building and pulled on the handle of the foyer door, but couldn't budge the heavy door, and the screaming continued. Mabel's frailties were no match for her determination; she gritted her teeth and muttered, "I'm coming! Hold your horses!"

She hooked her cane on her arm and with both hands pulled on the handle. She reared back on her heels, until her toes were nearly vertical, and as the door eased open, she slipped a foot around the door and wriggled into the foyer. She repeated the process with the second door and stumbled into the room with the pool.

Sure enough, Ruthie Sue was cringing in the corner, yelping like a wounded coyote. "What on earth?" Mabel asked the woman in the skimpy pink swimsuit.

Ruthie Sue covered her eyes with one hand and pointed toward the pool. "It's a snake—a poisonous water moccasin!" The sobs had subsided long enough for her to explain, but now they were billowing up like a summer thunderstorm.

"Don't be absurd. How could a snake get into an indoor swimming pool?" Mabel stepped brazenly to the edge. She scanned the pool a moment and to her amazement saw a small black reptile rippling across the surface, a shimmering wave in its wake. It had a yellow band around its neck and was about 13 inches long. "I can assure you, it is not a water moccasin."

"But, it"s alive!" Ruthie Sue slumped into a chair and hid her face in her towel. "Call 911," she blurted between sobs.

"First, I will dispose of the dragon and then I'll call the office, if it is necessary. I am sure they heard your screams! Cover yourself with your robe, for pity's sake." Mabel laid her cane on the concrete floor and grabbed the pool net, nearly losing her balance. "Poor little thing, he is more scared than you are!"

The door opened and standing, gawking at Ruthie

Sue and Mabel, were the head of security, the Executive Director, the Director of Health Care, superintendent of maintenance, and the pool manager, followed by Nurse Mary, pushing a wheel chair. Mabel commanded, "Kindly take care of the Loch Ness Monster." She pointed disdainfully to the snake and handed the net to the open-mouthed pool manager.

Good, Mabel thought, *I'll have something interesting to tell my daughter at lunch.*

ꕤ

Mabel paused long enough to close the apartment door. "The man across the hall is crazy," she whispered, nodding at room 403, with the nameplate: Dr. Tucker Quick.

"Who? Dr. Quick? I like him," Charlene replied, also whispering. "He smiles at me and speaks when I see him in the hall."

"He really is a nut. He keeps telling me I need a cat." Mabel spoke a bit louder as they moved toward the elevator. "He even offered to buy me a cat. Wait a minute, dear. Let me fix something." She stood on her tiptoes to tuck a blouse label under the collar of Charlene's green sweater.

Charlene shook her head. "Once a mother, always a mother."

"Until we die. Those trousers make you look even taller."

Mabel was not as tall as her daughter, but she had a regal presence—back straight, chin held high. Her nearly black eyes contrasted nicely with her white hair. Both ladies were slender.

"I'm going to have to take you to lunch more often,"

Charlene said. "You are getting much too thin."

"I've always been thin, dear."

Each thought the other was the more beautiful. "Did you check to see if my hair is messed up in back?" Mabel asked.

Charlene pulled a comb out of her purse. "It is just flattened where you leaned back against the chair. You have always been vain about your hair." She fluffed her mother's hair, and patted it down. "I love it white. Glad you gave up the hair color."

Their dispositions were alike—each had a "take charge" personality and they each called the other "bossy." Sometimes, they clashed, but they adored each other.

Shoving the comb into her pocket, Charlene held the elevator door open while Mabel, leaning gingerly on her cane, stepped in. "If your new neighbor is such a nut, why don't you introduce him to Ruthie Sue?"

"Well! He's not *that* crazy. Do I have a story to tell you!"

Charlene smiled. "I think you like him, Mother."

Mabel fiddled with a button on her purple sweater. "The tale I am going to share is not about him. It's about Ruthie Sue and the pool. Dr. Quick is okay, but he's a bit looney! And why would I want a cat on the 4th floor, no less."

As the elevator slowly descended, Charlene asked, "Have you baked your cherry chocolate cake for him yet?"

"Humph! You act like I am trying to make an impression on the nut."

Charlene tossed her long red hair back over her shoulder. She was laughing hard when the elevator opened into the lobby.

"Behave yourself, child, or I won't go to lunch with you. And by the way, he knew your father."

"Dad? When? Where?"

"They were in graduate school together at Wake Forest. Probably 60-65 years ago. I'll let him tell you about it."

"When?"

"He's coming over for pie and coffee about two o'clock."

Charlene ducked her head. "Un, huh," she muttered under her breath.

ꟸ

At exactly two o'clock, there was a tapping at the door. *Well,* thought Mabel, *at least Tucker has one good attribute. He is prompt!* He handed Mabel a pink rose.

"You do not have to bring me a flower, Tucker, but thank you and come in to meet my daughter."

Tucker smiled. "A rose is fair exchange for your baking." He turned to face Charlene and for a moment just looked at her. "I'll bet your father called you 'Charlie,'" was his opening remark. "And you got his red hair. Delightful!"

"How did you know he called me Charlie?"

"Well, his first name Charles, even though he went by Davis, right? He called me 'Tuckie' once—when he wanted a black eye."

"Sit down, Dr. Quick. Mom has baked a wonderful pie," Charlene said.

Mabel was busy finding a bud vase but she heard his response: "Yep, she is good about that. Trying to make an old man fat."

"Dear, if you come serve the coffee, I'll handle the

pie," she said to her daughter. "Tucker, do you want to come to the table?"

"Let's sit in the living room, Mabel. If I stay too close to the pie, I'll gain five pounds."

When they were seated, Tucker said, with a serious face, "I'm going to have to move."

"No, Tucker! Not really," Mabel said. "Are you kidding us?"

"I'm going to have to move if I keep getting into trouble over here. You are too great a cook."

Charlene laughed and dribbled coffee on her blouse.

Tucker quickly offered her his napkin. He was not a handsome man, but he had a round, jovial face with deep wrinkles where he once must have had dimples. His gray eyes held a ready twinkle.

Mabel noticed that they had both saved her favorite blue chair for her. Watching them together, she realized they were already engaged like old friends. Often Charlene was so much like her father, she thought as she handed Tucker the chocolate pie with whipped cream. She leaned back in her chair and ignored her dessert. She had an unexpected joy in seeing them share anecdotes with each other, both of them remembering a great man and bringing him back to life for a few moments. It was good for Charlene to be reminded about how gifted and kind her father was.

"I know that sometimes he didn't have lunch money because he had bought a meal for someone else the day before," Tucker told them.

Charlene asked, "Doctor Quick, didn't you think my dad was brilliant?"

"Yes, but of course, he copied my test answers."

"Oh, yes, I'm sure!" Charlene chuckled. "How did you

know that Mother was his wife?"

"I have never met another Peterman—several Petersons but not Peterman. We managed to keep up with each other for 20 years or so. We were invited to their wedding but couldn't go. Dorrie and I lived out of the country for a few years."

Mabel said, "I had not met you but I remember how disappointed Davis was that you and Dorrie could not come to the wedding."

"We should have kept up with each other. I always regretted that we lost touch."

"My dad was not as big as you are."

"Nope. I'm just a homely old farm boy. Davis was handsome. Then, we both had hair—mine the color of a Labrador Retriever, his the color of an Irish Setter."

Mabel chimed in, "Not too many farm boys earn a PhD in Foreign Languages."

"Officially, my degree is in Linguistics, but, that was another life." He was quiet for a minute then reminisced, "My wife, Dorrie, was a tiny little thing." He stared out the window.

"I'll bet she was lovely," Charlene said.

Dr. Quick's voice was husky. "She was the most wonderful woman in the world.

We were married 61 years!" He caught himself and laughed. "Dorrie was much nicer to me than my neighbor from across the hall. I can tell you that!"

"Then," his neighbor said, "Maybe I'll not offer you another piece of pie."

"Well, *sometimes,* she's nice!" Dr. Quick said and gave Mabel a big smile.

ഗ്രൂ

Mabel had lived in the retirement home for two years. Her daughter and son convinced her to move there after she fell, twisted her knee and broke her hip. She had protested—loudly—at first, but she had come to enjoy her little apartment and its balcony that captured the morning sun. Yet as beautiful as her new situation was, not a day went by that Mabel failed to think of the mountains. Would she ever get used to the "flatlands"?

She missed her dog, Jeeves, terribly, but her son had adopted him and brought him to her apartment often.

The services of the community: the staff, the medical backup, the varied activities and all the other amenities made the move worthwhile. The Executive Director, Mrs. Devereux Strickland was known as "Dev" to both staff and residents and was greatly admired and respected. Why did she resist the move here? Why did so many older people fight moving to such a facility? Most people waited too long to enjoy the freedom found from living in a Continuing Care Retirement Community. It was not only the staff, but the other residents that kept her looking forward to each day. What extraordinary people she had met at Dogwood Glenn.

The greatest advantage of the move, of course, was that she was closer to Charlene and Ed and their families.

She had enjoyed a good day—if she could forget the swimming pool fiasco. She always enjoyed being with Charlene. Mabel had lived a wonderful life, she reminded herself, as she poured a cup of tea and carried it to the table beside her chair. Twice widowed, she cherished memories of two wonderful marriages, one for 32 years and the other for 18. She had two lovely children and five grands—plus three step-sons and their families. All of them spoiled her outrageously and she loved it. Yes, life had been good to her! She flipped on the sports channel on the television and leaned back in her chair. Two minutes later, she was sound asleep.

ꙮ

Charlene was worried about her mother. Her health seemed improved, except for her knee, but she was allowing Ruthie Sue to take up far too much of her time and energy. Mabel had a habit of collecting oddball friends to care for, and no one was more of an oddball than Ruthie Sue. Charlene knew Ruthie Sue telephoned her mother at all hours of the day and night and expected help in making the slightest decision.

Just a day or two before, her mother had told her someone was persecuting Ruthie Sue at the swimming pool. A mysterious "someone" had turned off the lights in the dressing room while she was taking a shower. Later, she claimed that "someone" had released a large number of big spiders in the shower stall. Gevano, the pool manager, had come to her rescue and killed the spiders. He had found only two. Now Ruthie Sue was refusing to shower in the Wellness Center. More recently, Ruthie Sue had found trash scattered around the room and into the pool, and Gevano had all but accused her of putting it there—according to Ruthie Sue.

"Where was the pool manager all this time?" Charlene asked.

"Oh, he takes his job very seriously. He checks the chemicals three times a day and the water is always crystal clear. He is as baffled as I am. You have seen him. Six-feet-four, dark hair and eyes. He is incredibly polite and helpful. I think half the residents are trying to introduce him to their granddaughters. But, I had a bad premonition," she continued. "I've seen Manuel's new helper fooling around the pool. I've seen that kid somewhere else before."

Why was her mother engaged with the pool at all? She didn't swim—didn't even own a suit. She sat beside the pool and did the crossword puzzles each morning while Ruthie Sue did water aerobics. Mom insisted that no one else would go to the pool with Ruthie Sue and no one was allowed to go alone.

"Why don't you at least get in the water, Mother?" Charlene asked. "You went to the pool and enjoyed it after Dad's stroke. You participated in the whole rehab program with him. It might help your bad knee and hip."

"Your dad is not here now," her mother had said, "and I looked a tad better in a swim suit 25 years ago than I would now. Also, I take physical therapy for my knee."

Charlene reminded herself that her mother was surrounded by a host of lovely, caring, mature friends in the community and she decided not to worry. Of course, there was also Tucker Quick.

Her mother had been devastated at the death of Charlene's father. They had been as close as any couple she had ever known and were exemplary role models for their son and daughter. She had underestimated her mother's resilience because three years later she had married an old family friend, Will Yancey. That marriage appeared as blessed as the first and Mabel told her once that she couldn't possibly tell you that she loved one of her husbands more than the other. Charlene had been a bit offended at first. How could Will take the place of her father? He never tried to take his place, brought happiness to her mother, and was always a loving friend to the family. Would Tucker Quick become husband number three? No, she doubted it very much. They were friends and that was good. He was able to handle her mother's bossiness, but Mabel gave as well as she received and the two of them were hilarious together.

Chapter Two

Mabel leaned over the railing of her 4th floor balcony to watch as a moving van was being unloaded. It was larger than some of the vans and the workers were toiling over a huge piece of furniture.

She loved it when new residents came to Bougainvillea Hall—and this resident was moving directly below her. She retrieved her tall stool from the kitchen and sat down to observe. The workers, in green uniforms, seemed to be struggling with an unusually shaped piece of furniture. It was wrapped in blankets and appeared to be very heavy. They were being cautious with the mystery piece. She could not see as much as she wanted because the portico got in the way.

"Why, I think it is a piano!" Mabel said to her clematis plant. It had to be a baby grand with its legs removed. Mabel loved music and her favorite instrument was the piano. Her preferred trips every year were the ones when the Activities Director took a bus load of residents to the North Carolina Symphony.

Another worker joined the crew and they moved slowly toward the door. Mabel was positive that the instrument, even without legs, could not possibly fit into the elevator. *For heaven's sake, would they carry it up two flights of stairs to the 3rd floor?*

She left the balcony, grabbed her cane and hurried to the elevator. As it opened on the 1st floor, she faced a mover—whose grimaced countenance demonstrated the effort they were expending. Mabel squeezed her shoulders in and pushed closer to the corner. "How on earth are you going to get that thing in here?" she asked.

He shifted his load, almost sinking to his knees with its weight, and shuffled a little so she could get out. "Let me stay here so I can watch. I love pianos."

He smiled and nodded to her, which she thought might be a substitute for a bow, but protested. "Sorry, but there will barely be room for the piano."

Reluctantly, Mabel stepped out, but she stood where she could study the situation silently. Her daughter and granddaughter played the piano. She could hardly wait to tell them. She gasped when she saw the workmen turn the six foot long piano up on end, slowly maneuver it into the space and close the door. *Well, I'll be a monkey's aunt,* she thought.

She paused to wonder if she should wait and call the elevator back down, but her curiosity gave her a little nudge. She would take the stairs. The bannister felt firm and supportive. She ran her hand along the top of it, enjoying the smoothness of it as she pulled herself up. Using her cane in her left hand, she continued her journey. One flight.

On the landing of the second floor, she smelled smoke. But when she sniffed again, Mabel relaxed. *Dolly is burning toast again. Why does Todd let her cook?*

She knew the odor would linger for hours.

Half way up the next flight, she had to sit down on the stairs. Elena, one of the cleaning staff, was going down the stairs. "My gracious, Miss Mabel. Can I help you?"

"No, child. I'm just resting. Did you see if they got the piano into the apartment?"

"Is that what they were carrying? They were still in the hallway a moment ago."

Mabel had to catch her breath. She wished she had been a little quicker. The moving crew was not to be seen when she finally got to the top of the stairs. *Somehow they got the load into the apartment. Probably takes up the whole living room.*

She stepped discreetly into the hallway of apartment 304. They had the instrument on its side applying its legs. She wanted to shout, "Hallelujah!" There was a piano in her building and perhaps she could hear it being played.

A young woman, about Charlene's age, giving instructions as to location, saw her. "Come in," she invited.

"No, I must not bother—but who plays the piano?"

"Our whole family does but this one belongs to my mother Grace Guimares, who will be here tomorrow." She extended her hand. "I am Katlin Walker."

"I live right above. I hope I can hear your mother playing every day."

Katlin smiled and Mabel suddenly hoped she would visit often. "Then, will you do me a favor? Ask my mother to play. She has not been to the piano since my father died. She didn't want us to move the piano, but we think she needs it."

"What a shame. Had they been married long?"

"Fifty-six years."

"Well, I can understand, dear."

"You can?" Katlin stepped aside to let a mover by. "But it has been almost two years."

Mabel put her hand on the younger woman's arm. "My dear, when those of us who have loved for many years lose our mate, we do feel like the music has left our hearts."

Katlin wrinkled her brow at the imagery. "But she is a fine musician. Shouldn't it come back?"

Mabel cocked her head to study the younger woman. "Don't rush her," she urged quietly. "Until you have experienced it, you cannot understand. Just be patient and give her your love."

A look of relief and also one of reverence spread across Katlin's face. "Thank you so much. You sound so wise. You must be the lady the Wylers told us about. You know Dr. Sam and Dr. Stella? They have been friends of ours for many years."

"They are fine people. Fine people. Don't believe anything they told you about me! I'm not that bad! Just a little crazy."

Mabel was halfway down the hall when Katlin called to her. "Did yours come back? Your music?"

"Yes!" She turned toward the elevator, "Twice!"

ஐ

Two nights later Mabel answered the bell to find Grace and Katlin at her door. She had delivered Grace a packet of materials about the community and a half dozen of her butterscotch brownies.

"We need some telephone numbers," Katlin said. "The Wylers are not at home and we came to ask you."

Grace had as lovely a smile as her daughter. Mabel found her to be gracious and beautiful. "I have a daughter about your age," Mabel said to Katlin and invited them to have some tea and cookies.

"I would love to meet your daughter. I'll go back to work next week so I'll not be around as much to help Mom."

Grace bragged about how much help Katlin had been. "Does your daughter come see you often?"

"Not as often as I would like—but she has a family, a job and a life of her own. She lives in Cary. But, you will hear people complaining all the time because their family does not wait on them hand and foot. Why did we come here in the first place if it wasn't to make life easier on all of them?"

Katlin lived in Cary also and only a block or two from Charlene. "I'll call her and perhaps we can come together some day and take our mothers to lunch."

Chapter Three

Mabel heard the incessant ringing of the telephone, but she ignored it. Worn out from doctor and lab appointments, she retired early. Her family complained about the ridiculously early time she usually went to bed.

The clamor of the telephone was joined by a thumping on the door—that grew louder and stronger. *Mercy sakes! Is the building on fire?* She finally roused herself to lift her head and gaze at the clock. It was blinking. She couldn't see the dial of her watch. She pulled the phone to her ear, but it was dead. The banging on the door continued unabated. She reached for her flannel robe and staggered to the door. As she opened it, Tucker grabbed her arm.

"Wha-a-t?"

"Tornado warning," he said. "We must get to the first floor hallway." His attire was a grossly loud red and green robe with red slippers.

"Let me get my cane and comb."

"For crying out loud! Forget the comb, will you?"

"I will not!" She replied haughtily, "Go on if you are afraid. I'm awake now and can certainly find my way."

"Mabel! I have been downstairs once and when you were not there I came back to get you. Will it take the whole fire department to get you to safety?"

"I'm coming, Tucker. Right now."

Emergency lights, working off batteries, replaced the regular hall lights, a bit whiter and less bright than the regular lights. Rain slammed against the windows and bolts of lightning ripped the sky. White light zigzagged around the lobby like frenetic, demonical dancers. Mabel wanted to stop to watch the fireworks, but Tucker tightened his grip on her arm. "Down."

"Onto my knees?"

He grimaced and relaxed his hold a little. "I'm sorry. I didn't mean to hurt you. You are just too darn stubborn."

"No," she responded and giggled. "You are stubborn. I am persistent."

As they moved across the lobby, they were joined by Marylouise McCoy, sleepily trying to button her robe. She hurried toward the elevator.

"No, Marylouise," Tucker said. "Don't use the elevator. It might be unsafe."

Mabel exclaimed, "We are on the fourth floor! I cannot walk down three flights of stairs."

Tucker sounded exasperated. "I'll help you. Both of you."

Marylouise thanked him but brushed his hand aside. "You'll have your hands full with Mabel." She clung to the bannister and they began their descent.

Her statement might have irritated Mabel, but tall, stately Marylouise never seemed to need help. She was a retired art teacher and owned an art gallery.

"Wait for me!" The yell came from Lloyd Ray Oliver. "Should I bring my cat?"

Marylouise paused and turned back. "I'd better get my canary."

"Your fool cat and canary can take care of themselves. Now, shake a leg or we will all be killed." Tucker didn't try to hide his annoyance.

"People," Mabel explained, "we will not all be killed. Tucker is just chomping at the bit. His patience has worn thin."

"But it seems unreal. It gives me an eerie feeling to be going down the stairs in the middle of the night with everyone wearing their night clothes!" Marylouise said.

Tucker replied, "Just pretend it's a costume party."

"Wait," Lloyd Ray said, "where's Hilda?"

"For crying out loud. Hilda is already downstairs. So is everyone else who has any brains. They are probably all sitting on the floor telling tall stories about the horrors of some tornado they bravely lived through. We have to move!" Tucker took Mabel's arm again and escorted her toward the next flight.

"Tucker," Mabel whispered, "did you really come back up just for me?"

"Don't make me regret it, old lady."

Mabel giggled again. "I thank you, old man." She was feeling light-headed.

On the third floor landing, they were met by the Wylers—Dr. Sam and Dr. Stella.

They looked dressed for a medical convention in business suits. Dr. Sam carried his black medical bag and each of them had a huge flashlight.

Tucker asked, "Expecting to deliver any babies here tonight?"

"Never can tell. I remember once—"

Dr. Stella took his arm. "Hurry up, Sam."

A few other stragglers joined them on the second

floor; several dressed in street clothes but some of them in sleep apparel. A few of them seemed to be enjoying the flight. Others were clearly frightened to death.

On the first floor, Mabel was relieved to see that the residents had pulled chairs from their apartments and the lobby. The thought of sitting on the floor had distressed her all the way down. She sank into an upholstered chair. "Now, where is the hot tea?" she joked. She looked around to count all the residents from her floor. "Where is Lucas Pullen?"

"Well, I'm not going back up to hunt for him," Tucker said.

"I hear the elevator," Mabel told him. Indeed, it opened and out stepped Lucas, complete with a huge bag of popcorn. He wore short pants and a pink shirt that was still unbuttoned. His bald head matched his shirt and he was smiling and nodding at everyone.

"And what was the problem with the elevator?" Mabel asked Tucker, and her sarcasm was not missed.

"Why, Miss Mabel, you wore your sleeping bonnet," Lucas said.

Mabel touched her hair and shrieked. She jerked off her purple bouffant hairnet and faced Tucker. "Why didn't you tell me? I look like an idiot in this thing!"

"I thought it was cute," he replied, grinning.

"Cute is not my way." She turned her back on Tucker.

At the far end of the hall, someone had a radio tuned to the weather station and a group gathered around, intent on following the progress of the storm. A few residents seemed terrified, but the excitement gave cause for several to begin their tall tales of killing storms. Strangely, Mabel thought they acted like they were gathering for a party. She worked on her hair and rubbed her sore knee.

She looked for the newest resident, Grace Guimares. Dr. Stella was with her, and further down the hall, Dr. Sam was taking Ruthie Sue's blood pressure. Stella had pulled her gray hair back into a pigtail, but some hair had pulled loose and gently framed her face. She was a little taller than her husband. He was kind, loving, serious, and he had a head full of white, wavy hair—the archetypical family doctor.

Todd Hartford was consoling his wife Dolly, who held her small, shivering toy Chihuahua on her lap. She fretted about the danger the dog faced and the possibility that she would be carried away by the tornado. They were an unusual couple. Todd was tall—very tall, and thin. He had taught math in junior high school and was very talkative. Dolly was short, had clipped black hair and was a quiet, unassuming person.

Lucas was passing his popcorn around, much to the distress of Arlene Snider. Mabel considered Arlene a health nut. She was neat and attractive even at this unholy hour. She had owned a health store. "You are messing up your cholesterol, Lucas," Arlene said.

"My what?"

Mabel couldn't hear Arlene's answer but she saw the disgust in Tucker's expression. *Was he annoyed with Arlene, or was it because Lucas didn't know what cholesterol was?*

Mabel's cursory check revealed that all the residents were accounted for, even the very quiet Noah Malone. He was sitting near Rachelle Moffitt who was, as usual dressed to the hilt, or as Tucker said, "loaded for bear." Her brown slacks and blouse were accented by a wide gold belt and four or five gold chains shining against her blouse. She looked as if she had just stepped out of the beauty parlor. She had been an opera and stage star.

Tucker was making his rounds, encouraging and teasing his neighbors. Mabel wished he would come back and sit near her.

Lucas pulled a couple of energy bars out of his shirt pocket. "Want one, Mabel? I'm too tired to chew them."

"Some energy bars. Maybe if you ate one, it would give you the energy to eat the other one. Offer one to Arlene," she suggested and watched to see her reaction.

Lucas came back very quickly, his face and bald head red. He unwrapped one of the bars and ate it. Mabel was not sure what his occupation had been but, probably, he was a salesman. He had the personality for sales.

Mabel didn't ask him what Arlene had to say. On the whole, she thought everyone was behaving remarkably well, but she was eager for an all-clear announcement.

The rain turned to hail, pounding windows in the lobby. There were several audible complaints about the hail denting automobiles. A strange expectancy grew in the hall, people sitting a bit straighter as if they were responding to a dramatic change in pressure. Mabel felt like all the air had been sucked out of the room and she felt like her head was going to explode. The battery powered emergency lights flickered and one of them went out. A supernatural silence filled the space—like the sudden stopping of thunderous applause. Then they all—even the hard of hearing—heard the roar, like a jet airplane taking off over them followed by an awesome sound of crashing and twisting of metal and glass. Everyone spontaneously and simultaneously ducked.

As fast as it came, the wind and noise were gone and the resulting deadly quietness unnerved Mabel. The stunned residents began to stir.

"Ruthie Sue fainted," someone called, and Dr. Sam hurried to her aid.

Dolly began to bawl. "Baby is gone! The twister carried my Baby away!"

She, however, was drowned out by Etta Worthington's scream: "Something is under my skirt!"

Todd had his hands full but as Etta stood up, Baby emerged from under her skirt. "Dolly," he said, "the rat is alive." He sounded a bit regretful.

Etta was horrified. A retired kindergarten teacher, she wore, as always, a full, gathered skirt that made her look a bit squatty.

Tucker and Lloyd Ray were the first to check for damage. "Heavens to Betsy!" Lloyd Ray exclaimed, "The whole portico is gone!"

Tucker held up his hand. "You ladies wait here until help arrives. All the glass and metal and boards could be dangerous." He disappeared into the former lobby.

"If anyone has a cell phone, call 911," Lloyd Ray said.

Mabel looked across the lobby just in time to see Lloyd Ray slip on storm debris and fall backwards. Marylouise shot out of her chair to race to him. He lay on the floor, his face bleeding, and lying very still.

"Dr. Sam! Dr. Stella! Come quickly!" Mabel called.

Marylouise knelt on the floor beside Lloyd Ray. Mabel was not surprised at Marylouise's reaction but she had not realized that their friendship had developed so far. She put her hand on Marylouise's shoulder. "Dr. Sam is coming and also the paramedics."

Lloyd Ray was stirring now and Marylouise was using her handkerchief to wipe blood from his forehead. "I'll take care of your cat," she whispered.

"Why?" he asked dazedly.

"'Cause you might be going to the hospital." She moved so that Dr. Sam could get to him.

Mabel could hear running in the hall and saw the maintenance supervisor, James and the security officer, Joe coming with Nurse Mary following. James rushed into the lobby. "Is everybody accounted for?" Joe wanted to know. He was carrying a clip board with an apparent list of residents. He began a roll call and wandered around the group making checks on his list.

Arriving next, the police and the paramedics required all residents to remain on the first floor while they did a systematic check of each apartment. The paramedics checked on Ruthie Sue and continued through the group, making sure everyone was okay. Only Lloyd Ray had been injured.

Grace asked James to please check to see if her piano was all right.

Mabel moved where she could see the lobby and was startled to see a tree—the beloved Bartlett pear tree—had been blown through the glass and lay in the middle of the lobby. She hoped the big maple near her apartment was all right.

The biggest concern the inspectors had was for the roof, but the extent of the damage was hard to determine in the dark. Most of the lower floor windows had been blown out.

James held up his hand and asked for attention. "Dev

will be here soon, but she has ordered cots to be set up in the hallway and in the administration building. Those of you on the west side, after your apartment has been inspected, might be willing to share beds in your apartments. If you do not have emergency candles, we will provide them."

Ruthie Sue asked Mabel to spend the night in her apartment.

"Let me have the couch and perhaps Archie and Kay can use your spare bedroom." Mabel insisted and she realized that she might pass out if she couldn't lie down soon. But, first, she had to find Tucker.

Tucker was with Lloyd Ray and Mabel could see it was unlikely the patient would be going to the hospital. Marylouise was still there, and Lloyd Ray was sitting in a chair pulled from the hallway and a paramedic dressed the cut on his forehead.

Tucker turned to Mabel. "Are you all right?" he asked as he studied her. "You look awfully tired."

"Yes, I'm both all right and tired. I'm going to Ruthie Sue's apartment. Where will you sleep?" she asked.

"You know I'm a night owl. I'll find a cot somewhere. You sleep well."

"Thanks, Tucker, for getting me down here."

"You are very welcome. It was my pleasure." He put his arm around her and gave her a friendly hug. "I'll walk you to Ruthie Sue's apartment."

Chapter Four

On her way home from shopping with Ruthie Sue at WalMart one morning, Mabel drove past Dolly Hartford standing on the corner of a busy intersection, holding her white Chihuahua.

They were miles from home, and Mabel was concerned because she knew about Dolly's propensity for getting lost, so Mabel circled the block. The police had returned Dolly to Dogwood Glenn several times, warning Todd that he had to take better care of her. Mabel had not talked to her since the tornado, when she thought her little dog, "Baby," had been carried away with the wind.

Mabel knew Todd was often at his wit's end, trying to care for an Alzheimer's patient. She wished she could help. Dolly was going downhill pretty fast, but Todd insisted on caring for her himself. She wore her usual tee shirt and knee length shorts, in spite of a brisk wind. She carried no purse and probably had no identification.

Mabel stopped and put down the window. "Dolly? Are you lost? Get in and we'll take you and Baby home." The dog was trembling, surely exhausted, and cold.

Dolly hesitated, clearly disoriented, and Mabel said, "I'm Mabel. I'm a neighbor. I live in Bougainvillea Hall also. This is Ruthie Sue. She lives on your floor."

Dolly nodded and opened the car door. "I don't know

where my husband is."

"I'll help you find him." Mabel drove toward Dogwood Glenn. "How is your little dog?"

"Fine." That was almost the total extent of her conversation. Mabel asked her how old Baby was. She shrugged her shoulders.

"How long have you and Todd been married?" Mabel asked. Again Dolly shrugged.

It was hard for Mabel to imagine that this shadow of a woman had once been the head nurse in a prestigious pre-natal surgical unit in a major hospital. As much as she enjoyed life, Mabel had to agree with friends that growing old was not for sissies.

Mabel had some experience with Alzheimer's Disease because she had watched her sister struggle—for years—to care for her husband. She knew it was a dementia that usually affected people over sixty. She also knew that more than five million Americans have the disease. She hadn't worried about it when she was sixty since only five per cent of people develop it by then; however, she recently read that sixty per cent of people over eighty-five come down with Alzheimer's disease. She found herself wondering about herself every time she lost her keys or forgot a name. Dogwood Glenn had an Alzheimer's Unit and Mabel had been pleased with what she learned about it.

All at once, Dolly said, "I used to drive."

"I did also," Ruthie Sue said. "But my car was hijacked and wrecked."

Dolly did not respond.

"Why don't you take the insurance money and buy a

new car?" Mabel asked.

"Someone might steal it. Anyway, I don't want another car."

Mabel frowned. "Ruthie Sue, you must not let that one episode cripple you for life."

"Have you ever had a knife held to your throat?" Ruthie Sue said, pouting. "Anyway, the thief has a family and some brother might come after me."

"Don't be silly, Ruthie Sue. No, you are right," Mabel agreed. "I have never been faced with a life-threatening experience in a criminal case, but I would not let it define my life."

When Mabel pulled into the parking lot in front of Bougainvillea Hall, Dolly seemed confused. "I don't know where we are," she said timidly.

"We are back at Dogwood Glenn. I'll show you to your apartment."

"But, where is Todd?" Dolly asked.

"I think we will find him in your apartment."

When she rang the doorbell, Mabel hoped, with all her heart, that Todd would be home. What could she do with Dolly if he did not answer the door?

He did. "Hello, Mabel. Where have you been, Dolly? You know you are never to leave the apartment by yourself."

"I couldn't find you," Dolly said as she released Baby.

"I do have to use the bathroom every once in a while. Where did you find her, Mabel?"

ഽ൭

Mabel had tried to take Dolly on a few short trips when the Hartfords first moved in last summer. When she took a group of friends to a local strawberry farm, she invited Dolly.

As soon as Dolly realized that the group was not going to pick their own fruit, she got back into the hot car and refused to buy any berries.

After they had been home an hour or so, Mabel discovered Dolly in the lobby.

"What are you doing?" she asked.

"A lady said she was going to take me to pick strawberries and I'm waiting for her."

Mabel felt a twist in her stomach. Dolly had been waiting for more than an hour in the lobby for her because she didn't realize that they were going to buy strawberries, not pick them. If she had not already scheduled a dental appointment, she would have gone back to the farm and picked berries with Dolly. Mabel didn't know how to explain the situation to her so she found Todd and told him. He promised to explain it. Mabel reminded him of the fine Alzheimer's Unit at Dogwood Glenn.

"That is one reason we moved here. But I want to take care of her as long as I can," Todd told her.

"I know. My brother-in-law had the disease and my sister attended him as long as she could, but it nearly killed her."

"I know that if the situation was reversed, Dolly would take care of me," Todd said.

It was a statement that Mabel had heard many times at Dogwood Glenn.

Chapter Five

Some might consider Mabel Yancey a "busy-body" and, she admitted to herself, she probably was, but it stemmed from her interest and concern for her friends and neighbors. She had been intrigued by the change in the upbeat attitude of Lucas Pullen for days and was glad to see him early one afternoon at the mailboxes.

"Lucas," Mabel greeted him, "you seem extra-ordinarily cheerful these days. Is there something going on that I need to know?"

Lucas startled her. He unexpectedly bowed from the waist, and his comb and glasses dropped to the floor from his shirt pocket. His bald head looked white against the gray of the narrow ring of hair he had left. She fought an almost irresistible urge to pat the shiny, round head. He picked up his comb and glasses, straightened up and grinned. "Yes, indeedy, Mabel! Arlene and I are working on some projects together."

Mabel found it difficult to believe that Arlene, a health nut, could work with Lucas, a fast food junkie, but she thought it might be interesting. She pulled the mail from her box. "What kind of projects? Is she making you give up your candy and popcorn?"

Lucas sounded flustered. "Yes, the candy and popcorn are a project but, also, we are starting a dance class and a water aerobics class."

Mabel tried to keep her surprise under control, afraid it showed in her voice, but to imagine these two together was a quick exercise in imagination. "How nice," she said. "I knew Arlene was interested in starting a fitness class but I never dreamed it would be in the water! Have you asked Ruthie Sue to the aerobics class?"

Lucas was beaming with pleasure. "She was the first to sign up. Haven't you seen our signs around the campus? Our first water class is tomorrow at 10 a.m. Why don't you come?"

"I don't think so. Not in a hundred years would I get into that pool."

"Aw, come on, Mabel. You would love it!" He touched her arm and she thought he was going to get emotional and hug her. She stiffened her spine.

"I might come with Ruthie Sue, just to watch. But, it's turning cold tomorrow."

"We'll be indoors in a heated pool. Can't beat that!" He pushed his key into the mailbox and pulled out his mail. "Shoot! All I ever get is catalogs and bills. I'll leave it here." He shoved the material back into his box. "I have to go set up a video arrangement. Good to talk with you!" He scurried toward the entrance.

Mabel closed the door to his mailbox. "Lucas! You may need these!" She held up the keys he had left in the lock.

He wasn't the least bit embarrassed. "I'm so scatterbrained lately."

"Perhaps you are in love." Mabel couldn't resist.

He didn't reply but his neck, face and even his bald head turned red. He took the keys without another word.

ꕥ

Mabel walked like a queen—back ram-rod straight, chin up—and she had little patience for poor posture. Shuffling along beside her, with shoulders drooping, chin hugging her chest, and dragging her swimming bag, Ruthie Sue looked like a lost puppy.

Mabel chided her. "Pull up your shoulders! Lift your chin! You walk as though you were on your way to the gallows."

"I can't help it, Mabel. My back hurts."

"Mine would also if I walked like you. If you had better posture, your back would probably feel better. Walk like you were really excited about this class!"

If Mabel expected a spectacle in the water aerobics class, she would get one—more than she dared hope for.

Ruthie Sue seemed anxious all the way to the Wellness Center. "Let's hope the door will open! It has a faulty catch and locks accidently if it is slammed."

Mabel took a seat on the far side of the pool where she would be out of the way. She had a book—for appearance sake—although she didn't intend to read.

Several people had to unlock the foyer door for late arrivals. Mabel thought of moving closer to the door so she could be the opener, but that was not the kind of task she enjoyed, and it was cold outside, so she sat where she was, observing participants coming in from the blistering cold, pulling off their jackets and caps and heading for the dressing rooms. She was surprised that twelve people showed up for the first class.

Well, she thought, when residents were ready for the pool, *I'm glad I had enough fortitude not to sign up and put on a shamefully skimpy swimming suit!*

The pool took up roughly two-thirds of the Wellness Center, and measured 40 by 20 feet. Above the pool two paddle fans circulated the air.

The dappled reflection of the sunlight played on the walls. The room was rather plain, but the management had decorated the walls with large yellow and white sunflower motifs, each with a large round mirror in the middle. They were hung at random heights on the south wall and Mabel was glad they had the discretion to hang them high enough not to reveal aging physiques that were better served with more clothes on. Mabel wished she had a case of the cream she had seen in an advertisement. It promised to wipe out wrinkles and to defy gravity. A lot of people here needed help with gravity, in the stomach, legs and chest areas. She had never seen so many women with lumpy and bumpy looking thighs and men with thin legs and big bellies. It could have been demoralizing to the group stepping cautiously into the blue-tiled pool, but they seemed to ignore mirrors and propriety. Where was their dignity? Perhaps she was just too prim.

Then, it occurred to her they were the brave ones. They cared more about doing something to improve their health than she did. They accepted well-used bodies that had served them for many years. She had a moment of shame—but just a moment. No way was she going to join them—not that she looked any better or worse than most of them.

The spa—most residents called it a hot tub—was built in an alcove at the eastern end of the building. The alcove was built in a pentagon shape and the five walls had floor to ceiling windows, flooding the area with sunlight on sunny days.

Anthony Green turned on the jets to the hot tub and climbed down into it. His wife looked aghast. "You said you would join the class!"

"No, I said I would go with you to the pool."

"That's disgusting," Ruby said and joined the group in the pool.

The bubbly sound of air jets in the hot tub, blended with the low humming of the ceiling fans, could have put Mabel to sleep, but the room was too hot. The sticky humidity made her clothes stick to her. She untucked the hem of her blouse. She hoped no one would notice but she was nearly sick with the heat. Gevano used bromine in the pool rather than chlorine, but there was still a damp smell and she was glad when the sun came out to reflect in the pool.

At the front of the pool, Lucas had set up a large TV screen and he was busy getting the aerobic video ready. When he nodded to Arlene, she climbed out of the pool with the agility of Sadie, Oliver's cat. She looked trim and fit and wore the only white swimming suit Mabel could remember seeing.

"All our movements will be easy but I wanted us to try them once before we start the video." She demonstrated several exercise steps that the class repeated. "Okay, Lucas, start the video."

Lucas pushed the button on the machine and he did a hand spring over the edge and into the pool, breaking the rules posted by management. Lucas seems to be enjoying a second adolescence, Mabel thought.

As the exercises started, Mabel looked for Ruthie Sue. She seemed to be enjoying every second of the class. She looked so pleased to have others in the pool with her.

But the sun's glare reflected in the pool and hurt Arlene's eyes. "I'm blinded by the glare and I forgot my sunglasses," she exclaimed.

"Use mine," Beckie said. "They're in my walker."

"I'll get them," Lucas said and was out of the water quickly.

"My walker is outside, on the porch," Beckie told him.

"I'll find them," Lucas promised.

Arlene gave him a huge smile. "While he's gone, let's try some more of these moves." She moved to the side of the pool where there was less reflected sunlight. "We are going to start with the Hamstring Curls. Stand facing the pool wall. Stand straight and gently bend your left knee, lifting toward the buttocks."

Oh, no! Mabel said to herself. *Lucas went out wearing no coat or shoes.* She also thought his little red suit was much too short. He was nearly naked and wet in a temperature that was hovering around freezing.

Mabel saw Lucas hold up the sunglasses and pull on the door. A look of disbelief crossed his face. He yanked on the door handle. *Good Lord, it's locked.* He began to wave, then pound on the door but with people bending left knees in rhythm to Arlene's instructions, no one in the pool paid any attention to Lucas. The water was churning with kicks and arm movements.

"The poor man is freezing!" Mabel stood up and began a painfully slow walk toward the door, but it took her longer than Lucas needed to be exposed to the elements. Mabel finally got the attention of Anthony in the hot tub. "Hurry! Quickly! Open the door for Lucas."

"What?"

Mabel was frantic. She had forgotten how terrible

the acoustics were in this room. The class was now busy bending right knees.

Lucas had been jumping and clawing at the door. Now his face was twisted into a grimace and he was hugging himself, and his shaking could have jarred his teeth out.

Then, in answer to her prayers, and just as Mabel reached the foyer, Gevano walked up behind Lucas with his key extended. As the door swung open, Mabel heard a high, shrill scream, like a wounded cat. Lucas rushed to her, shoved the glasses at her, sprinted toward the hot tub and leaped in.

A startled Anthony slid backwards, his face white with astonishment. He lost his footing and with a whoosh slipped under the water. When his head resurfaced, he sputtered and, leaning against the tiled wall, backed up the steps away from the intruder.

Lucas ducked his head. *Oh, my,* Mabel thought, *now he is going to drown himself!*

But, he, too, came up sputtering. He snorted loudly but showed no interest in leaving the warm water.

Movement in the pool ceased and suddenly, all eyes were on Mabel. She looked down at the glasses in her hand as if she wondered how they got there, then, she extended them toward Arlene.

"Where's Lucas?" Arlene asked.

Mabel pointed toward the spa. She thought, *There is no explaining this so I will not try. Let Lucas tell them what happened.*

Chapter Six

Mabel's life was crowded with friends and responsibilities—she allowed too many people to be dependent on her. She had a soft spot in her heart for residents who were confused by the complexities of growing old, but little sympathy for those who took it as a personal affront.

"At our age, you have to expect some senses to become impaired," she often pointed out, "eyesight dimmed, hearing dulled."

She had a sadness for a few residents—those who were planted at Dogwood Glenn by children who never called or visited. She knew one lady whose children complained about the cost of her medical care. "You are spending our inheritance," they whined.

"I'd like to stomp those self-centered people," she told Charlene. "But, I also know of several families who supplement their parent's stay here."

Whether teacher, salesman, nurse or whatever career a senior citizen had enjoyed, old age was still old age. Some could cope better than others. Mabel was determined to live her life with fun. There were appointments to keep, activities to enjoy and special friends to nurture. Some of her dearest friends and family members told her: "Slow down, you are not a spring chicken, you know." But, without all her involvements, life would seem empty to her. Adventures were important—even when she had to nudge them along.

She didn't drive into town to the beauty shop, but rather, walked across the street to the small shop in the administrative building. The operators served independent residents as well as people from health care and the memory unit.

Mabel had heard Hattie Underwood, from the memory unit, complaining because the beauty shop had no name. So, playfully, Mabel printed one. She used her best calligraphy and penned a sign for the shop.

Y'all Come Deluxe Beauty Salon

She attached it with tape to the glass door. Raymie Trent, the hair dresser, loved it. Raymie's dark hair was a sharp contrast to Mabel's white. She always smelled faintly of gardenias and Mabel loved her perfume. She was already under the hair dryer when she saw Hattie at the door. As Mabel usually did, she raised the dryer a small amount so she could hear Hattie's remarks.

Hattie had more on her mind than the sign. "What have you done to me?" she asked Raymie. "What have you *done?*" She sounded desperate and Raymie was at a loss. "My hair and my eyebrows!" Hattie shrieked.

"I don't understand," Raymie finally managed.

"My hair! My hair! It was not white. You bleached my hair!" She tugged at Raymie's apron. "I had amber hair—beautiful amber hair—and you ruined it."

Mabel was afraid Hattie might attack the hair dresser. "Hattie," she exclaimed, raising the dryer higher, "your hair has been white ever since you came to Dogwood Glenn."

"It has not! I think I will sue you," she said and glared at Raymie.

Raymie backed into her counter. "Don't you have a picture? Let me see your driver's license."

Mabel turned off the dryer so she could hear.

"Okay, I'll show you." Hattie fumbled in her purse, pulled out a red wallet and fingered through it until she pulled out a long expired driver's license.

Raymie looked at it and held it so Mabel could see it. "Your hair is white in this picture," Raymie pointed out.

Hattie looked at the license. "Why, that's not me! I don't know who that old woman is."

"Hattie, I could put a rinse on your hair and make it amber again." Raymie said.

"You'll never touch me again!" She hurried to the door, walked out and slammed it. Then, while Mabel and Raymie were still staring at each other, she flounced back to the door, opened it and yelled: "I hate this stupid sign!"

When she slammed the door this time, the sign fluttered to the hallway floor.

"Slow-consuming age that changes us and confuses us takes its toll," Mabel quoted, but she couldn't remember whom to give credit to. "I guess it happens to the best of us. I'm so sorry she treated you that way, dear," Mabel soothed.

"Oh, she comes up with something every week. Last week she called me a bitch."

"Why do you work on her?"

"She won't remember what she said today. Poor soul," Raymie said. "I'll get old someday. I try to be patient. Most of my clients are wonderful."

Mabel said, "Growing old has one advantage; you

never have to do it again."

She tucked her head back under the dryer. "It takes a special person to work with us old people."

Raymie opened the door and reattached the sign. She was laughing when she came back into the shop. When the other hair dresser came to work, Mabel was watching to get her reaction to the makeshift sign. Bette Bass stopped to read it. She entered the shop asking who had made it.

"I'll only tell you if you like it," Raymie said.

"I think it is hilarious. Let's frame it and hang it inside. Mabel, you are so funny!"

"Thanks a lot," Mabel said. "But Raymie didn't tell you I made it."

"I know you," Bette said and put her supplies away—her towels and other items. "I see Corinne is late again." She fluffed up her own blond hair.

At that moment Corinne Newman, ignoring the sign, came into the shop with a flurry. She didn't speak to anyone in particular but announced, "Just wait until you hear all about my trip to Florida."

Mabel knew Corinne only slightly. She understood she had moved to Dogwood Glenn from Washington, D.C., and was recently divorced. Her children were out of state and rarely visited her. She had moved to the area to be closer to her only sister; however, her sister died in a car wreck shortly after Corinne moved south.

Corinne put down her purse and knitting bag and walked, already talking about her trip, to the shampoo chair. Bette turned the water up full force, but it could not lessen the irritation of Corinne's hoarse voice that droned on and on. Bette and Raymie exchanged glances and each shrugged. Corinne rambled about her trip the entire time Bette shampooed her hair and never pausing for breath, she continued the travelog as Bette set it. "So I said why am I in Florida if I don't go to Disney World?"

Mabel sighed. *Never mind that no one could care less about Corinne's trip. She must be a very lonely woman. Perhaps she will fall asleep under the dryer.*

Over the hum of the dryer, Corinne continued her monologue. Mabel grew weary of the garrulous prittle-prattle of a one woman talkathon. *Her talkfest reminds me of someone who is terribly afraid. She is scared to death of something. I must make an effort to get to know her better.* There was no interrupting the flowing tongue now, so she didn't try. When Corinne seemed to run out of steam, she picked up *The News and Observer* and read aloud the entire editorial page.

Raymie helped Mabel from the dryer and as she combed her hair, she noted: "Did you notice that Corinne didn't make eye contact with anyone? She just started talking a blue streak."

They tried to ignore the oral reading. "I wonder if she realizes that no one is listening to her." Mabel said.

"Somehow, I don't think it even matters to her."

When they missed the sound of Corinne's voice, they saw she had fallen to sleep under the dryer. The silence was a blessed relief, Mabel thought. Raymie said, "Do you remember that I told you that some of my clients talk to me about death? Well, Nettie is coming next and I wish you would talk with her."

"How will I broach the subject?" Mabel asked.

"Don't worry. She'll mention it."

When Nettie saw Mabel she asked, "Do you think

about death often?"

"I certainly do not dread it. Do you?"

Nettie rubbed her hands together. "The doctor wants to put me on an anti-depressant."

"I see nothing wrong with the medicine if you need it, but why don't you come to my apartment this afternoon and we can talk about your fear. I'll explain to you why you do not need to be afraid."

Nettie almost pulled her out of the chair in her attempt to hug her. "Oh, thank you, thank you, Mabel. I'll be there."

It worried Mabel that there were other residents who were frightened. Death was a part of living here. In a large continuing care community, old people get sick and die.

But to spend your last years worrying about dying? That was not for her. Life was much too short to live in fear. She needed to invite Nettie to her Bible Study Group. Her own faith had carried her through many years. She thought of one of her favorite hymns, "Victory in Jesus."

Chapter Seven

Mabel served as the member of the Resident's Council from her building at Dogwood Glenn and part of her job was to be helpful to newcomers. When Olga Wegener, a new resident from New York City called, just as Mabel started icing her cupcakes, she was polite.

"There's a man at my door," Olga said, "who wants to come into my apartment and change a filter of some kind."

"Does he have a Dogwood Glenn name tag?" Mabel asked as she tasted some of her frosting and decided it needed more vanilla.

"Yes."

"Then, he is legit. Let him in."

"But, Olga hesitated, "he's, uh, he's—"

Mabel ran down a mental list of the maintenance crew at the facility. "Is he in your apartment?" she asked.

"No! I made him wait in the hall while I called you."

Mabel chuckled to herself. "Well, he can't change the filter from the hall. I don't understand why you won't let him in." She tasted her icing again—*just right.*

"Well, Mabel, he's uh, uh—"

"Black?" Mabel fumbled with the vanilla bottle.

"Well, yes." Olga struggled, "And his hair looks awful creepy."

"Is his hair braided in dreadlocks?"

"I guess that is what you could call it. Ugh!" Olga interjected.

"Olga, that is Barry Phillips. Let him in. If you are frightened, although, I can't for the life of me know why you would be frightened of Barry, go to the lobby, or come up here."

"I'm afraid that if I left, there would be nothing here when I got back."

Mabel was losing her patience. "Don't be silly. Barry is to be trusted. He works here during the day and is going to college at night. He might be your physician some day."

"Not mine! He's … he's … well, he is—."

"Black?" Mabel repeated. "Or you could say African American. He is a Negro and a fine one. You probably used to call him colored. You know, I suppose, that the President of the United States is black."

"But—"

"Olga, you must live a bleak existence. Do what you want to do. I'm busy. But, if you want your air conditioning to work this summer, I would advise you to let him in. Then tell him to come up here for some of my lemon cupcakes. They are a favorite of his." She swiped a finger in the icing and tasted it again.

ꕥ

Mabel would have liked to avoid Olga a few days, but early the next morning she called her. "Are you free for a few moments?"

Olga replied, "I'm not doing anything that can't wait."

"Then meet me in the second floor lobby as soon as possible. You need to recognize some of the real dangers of living in the South." Mabel waited at the window and when Olga arrived she asked, "Do you know Josephine Keaton? She lives in Delphinium Hall."

"Is she the one who is always so depressed?"

"Yes," Mabel explained. "She's a trial to all of us. She was sitting on that bench over there under the oak tree and her sunbonnet blew away."

"Isn't that the man who came to my apartment? He is running after it. You told me I could trust him." Olga sounded quarrelsome.

"Did I really?"

"He's got the hat," Olga noticed. "Why, he seems to be returning it to her."

"Well, I'll be. He surely is!"

They watched as Barry playfully placed the hat on Josephine's head. A sudden burst of wind nearly sent it airborne again, but she held on to it, finally placing it in her lap. Laughing, Barry knelt beside her. He put his arm around the back of the bench.

"What's he doing to that old lady?" Olga asked.

"I think it is what's he doing *for* her," Mabel said.

"Isn't she afraid?"

"Does she seem frightened to you? She seems to be patting his arm. Thanking him, I suspect."

"Isn't he supposed to be working?"

Mabel replied, "I'm sure that taking care of a resident is part of his job description. He has carried a lot of groceries in for me."

Josephine bent her white head next to Barry and they could see that a serious conversation was going on. Mabel noted the white hair touching the black dreadlocks Barry wore. A sudden gust of wind began waving the tree branches and as the clouds deepened, it began to rain. Barry made a hand signal to Josephine, unmistakably telling her to wait. He ran to nearby car and returned with a red umbrella, which he held above her head, as he accompanied her to the administrative building.

Mabel said, "I'll see you later, Olga."

Olga stood staring out the window. "Oh," she muttered.

Chapter Eight

Professor Edward Peterman of the Math Department, State University, and a colonel in the Army Reserve, had trouble controlling his foot on the accelerator on his trip to see his mother. Today he had invited her to ask a guest to join them for lunch and she had called Dr. Tucker Quick. Edward was delighted and amused. This man's name was cropping up more often in their telephone conversations.

Ed had heard Dr. Quick speak years ago and he thought his book, *The Code Breakers* was a masterpiece. It had inspired his interest in cryptology. He had no idea that the old man was still alive. He must be approaching 90. Ed reached over and touched his copy of the book. He was hoping he could entice the author to autograph it.

Ed stepped from his car and followed the same pattern he always used, because he knew his mother was watching from the 4th floor balcony. He waved to her and then reached back into the car for Jeeves. He had to hold the dog down, as usual, as he attached the leather leash.

Jeeves looked up and Mabel began to clap and call to them. Ed could never convince her that he could not hear her above the din of traffic. The dog took off, but Ed was ready and managed to restrain him as he raced toward the new portico which was still under reconstruction. He was amazed that his mother had been sitting only yards from the damaged area when the tornado hit.

Ed had to pull back on the leash as they approached workmen who were repairing the recent damage. He had been a bit perturbed when her husband Will bought the King Charles Spaniel for his mother. He knew how active spaniels usually were and Jeeves lived up to the reputation when he was with Ed's family, but he showed remarkable restraint with Mabel. He had probably saved her life when she fell in her garden and broke her hip. He had alerted neighbors who called the rescue squad. He was a beautiful dog; white with brown and black patches and huge, soulful, black eyes.

A workman held up his hand to stop Ed. "Be careful of the debris."

"Thank you, I will," Ed said as he reached down to make Jeeves sit. "I followed the path of the tornado and am amazed that so little damage was done to this building. I had no idea that so many trees were taken out."

"It is amazing. Someone must have been praying. But. you should have seen it two weeks ago. It seemed to kinda skip along through this neighborhood. The main damage was about thre miles north of here."

As the elevator approached the 4th floor, Jeeves whined and wagged his tail. Ed released the leash and, true to his habit, the dog raced around the corner and straight toward Mabel's apartment. Mabel was always ready with the door open. She knew he would inspect each inch of the apartment, including the balcony, so she had that door open also. He always followed the same routine before he found his place beside Mabel's chair, where he would sit, content to rest his head on her lap, the whole time of the visit.

This time, however, Jeeves broke with protocol. Lloyd Ray Oliver, who lived at the far end of the hall, opened his door carrying his Maltese cat, Sadie, and set her down just as the dog reached Mabel. Jeeves sniffed her hand then tore down the hallway. Sadie arched her back, stood on tiptoes, screeched, then leapt to Lloyd Ray's shoulders. As Jeeves approached Lloyd Ray, Sadie vaulted from his shoulders and bolted down the hall, with the dog in hot pursuit, with Ed following yelling at him to stop. Mabel moved into the fray, waving her cane and shouting, "Catch him, Ed!"

Lloyd Ray was screaming, "No! No! No!"

Sadie veered to the right into the lobby and sprang to the top of a sofa, running along it and on to an upholstered chair and ascended to the 50 inch TV. She skidded across it, knocking a ceramic eagle and a vase to the floor. She then hopped to another sofa, ran along it and on to a table, spilling a bouquet of yellow roses and drenching Jeeves. From there, Sadie made a flying jump to a book case, dislodging knickknacks and an antique lamp. Tucker, hearing the commotion, stepped into the hall and barely managed to catch the lamp before it hit the floor.

Ed knew Jeeves had not touched the cat, but he was sure he was seeing gray fur flying everywhere. He was afraid Sadie might pounce on his mother and he ran to intercept the cat as she fled back down the hall. Sadie bypassed the two and sprinted into the apartment. She ran straight to the balcony and Ed quickly closed the glass door behind her.

"Whew!" Mabel said. She sank into her chair and Ed

thought she looked as exhausted as if she had been chasing Jeeves by herself. The wet dog quit his barking and came to sit quietly beside her. "Naughty dog," she chided. "You are not polite, and now you smell like a wet dog!"

Tucker and Lloyd Ray stood in the doorway. "Lloyd Ray, you have met my son. Tucker, this is Ed Peterman. Tucker, Ed."

Ed stuck out his hand. "What a pleasure, Dr. Quick! I have really been looking forward to this visit. I think your book on cryptology is the quintessential masterpiece on encryptions."

"And I have looked forward to meeting you, Ed."

Mabel exclaimed. "Tucker, you have been holding out on me. I didn't know about your book."

Tucker looked Ed up and down. "I think you are the spitting image of your dad except you might be a wee bit taller. Mabel," he said, turning to her, "my dear, that book was another life ago."

Lloyd Ray had waited patiently for the introductions and now he moved to the balcony glass doors. "I'm afraid she might jump. I've built up barricades on my balcony."

"Forgive us, Lloyd Ray," Mabel said. "What do you want us to do?"

"Let me go get her." A fresh voice came from the hall doorway. Marylouise came into the room. "She's not afraid of me."

"Let's take Jeeves to my apartment," Tucker offered. Jeeves was not too eager and, with his soulful black eyes, kept entreating Mabel to intercede for him. She leaned down and petted him. "Jeeves, darling, it is only for a short time. You'll come back."

When Ed and Tucker returned to the apartment, Marylouise was sitting on the floor of the deck, and Sadie was taking tentative steps toward her. When she had the cat safely in her arms, Lloyd Ray shoved open the glass door. "I thought you didn't like cats," he said.

"I never said that. I just don't like cats close to my canary. Take her. She is going to make me sneeze."

"I'm trying to train her to a harness and leash," Lloyd Ray said.

"You'll never train a cat. A cat trains you," Tucker said. "My wife's cat had me well trained."

"I know what I can do to make up for all this turbulent behavior on the part of Mother's dog." Ed winked at Tucker. "We'll take everyone to lunch. My treat."

When the five were sitting comfortably at the Grape Vine, Ed asked, "Marylouise, did you say you have a canary?"

"Yes, his name is Beverly Sills."

Ed hesitated. "His name is Beverly Sills?"

"He has a beautiful voice and I didn't know he was a male until after I named him."

Marylouise looked at Tucker who was already laughing.

Tucker said, "I told her she should just change his name to George Beverly Shea and she could still call him Bev."

"You are the most brilliant man, Tucker," Mabel said. "Perhaps almost as smart as Lloyd Ray. Did you know Lloyd Ray was a computer expert, Ed? He still stays busy helping people with their computers."

"Anyone who can fix computers is far brainier than I am," Tucker conceded.

Ed said, "My wife will be jealous. She's been wanting to meet you, Tucker. She teaches at State also and had classes this afternoon."

"If she is half as lovely as Mabel says, I know I'll be crazy about her."

"And she is beautiful, too," Marylouise added.

Ed smiled at her. He turned to Tucker. "Tell me about knowing my dad." Then, he turned to the others at the table. "Forgive the family talk, but Tucker knew my father. They were in graduate school together."

Graciously, Marylouise said, "We'd love to hear what Tucker has to say."

"See," Tucker exclaimed, "they are trying to figure out what makes Mabel tick by finding out about her past. I didn't know her, but I knew her fine husband."

Ed grinned. "Well, good luck in trying to find out what makes Mother tick!"

Lloyd Ray beckoned to the waitress. "I'll buy our dessert so we can enjoy this even more."

Mabel noticed that before he left, Ed exchanged business cards with Tucker.

"It includes my HAM radio call. I'd really like to talk with you about a project I'm doing."

"If it is work, count me out, son," Tucker said but he sounded pleased.

Chapter Nine

"Tucker! Come quickly. I need you." Mabel sounded panicky as she phoned her neighbor.

"Have you fallen? Are you in your apartment?"

"I'm in the pool. Come at once. We need you. Now."

Tucker sighed. "Mabel, I'm not dressed—and I haven't had my coffee."

Mabel yelled into the phone. "Well, come anyway!"

"Are you really in the pool?" He was almost amused.

"Course not!" And she slammed the wall phone back into its cradle.

Tucker rubbed his ear. What now? He nearly fell over trying to put his legs into his comfortable old overalls and cramming his pajama tops into them. He shoved his feet into some well-worn loafers and ran—as fast as an 84 year old could run—toward the Wellness Center. He had not made his coffee and had left the milk on the counter. He was not in a good mood. *In the pool? He just might drown her.*

Mabel called to him as he opened the door. She wore lavender slacks and blouse and she was as dry as toast and just as cantankerous as usual. His annoyance turned to anger. He would have felt better if she had been sopping wet and her perfect coiffeur plastered across her face. She had the nerve to tell him to hurry.

Tucker had not spent much time at the pool and this room was hot and humid, unlike the fitness room where he sometimes worked out.

Across the back of the building was a glassed-in room called the Garden Room and beyond it there was an adjacent patio and garden.

Tucker joined Mabel at the edge of the pool. "What's all the hullabaloo?"

His stomach was beginning to feel nauseated. His blood pressure medicine was to be taken with food and he hadn't eaten. His throat felt restricted and he had trouble swallowing. He clenched his hands into tight fists.

"It's a body—*was* a body," she explained. He leaned over to peer into the water. There was no body floating face down in the pool! There was no body floating face up! He could see some straw and wondered why the pool was not cleaner. *Ruthie Sue must be behind all this!*

Mabel was patting the concrete. "See the water? Someone pulled him out and dragged him out the patio door. Come on. Quick! We'll have to find him."

Tucker scratched his head. "What's wrong with you? I'm going back to my apartment. There's no body. And if there had been, how did it disappear with you here watching?" *Rather than drowning her, I might just strangle her.* "Anyway, I'm never myself until after I have my coffee."

"Good. I'll enjoy you while I can. I know what you are like after coffee."

"Tisk, Tisk, Mabel, it's too early for sarcasm."

Mabel continued with pronounced patience: "When we saw the body, Ruthie Sue became very ill and started vomiting. I helped her into the dressing room to revive her and to clean her up. When I came out—well, you know the rest." She raced to the garden room entrance and was signaling with her cane for him to hurry. He did not like to be intimidated but, weak man that he told himself he was, he followed her.

She turned back and called across the pool. "Now you tell Gevano exactly what I told you to say."

Tucker saw Ruthie Sue emerging from the ladies dressing room. *Now I really need to go home.*

"Tucker," Mabel said. "Pay attention. We don't know who he is but he was wearing blue jeans and a checkered shirt."

Ruthie Sue was leaning against the wall, her body still shaking with gasps as she tried to control her sobbing. "They have a con-con-conspiracy against me, trying to drive me crazy," she said between sobs.

Tucker was too much of a gentleman to express the obvious. The acoustics in the room were terrible and her sobbing had an eerie, muffled sound.

"Dr. Quick, there really was a body," she said, sniveling.

"Yeah, sure. Right. And he got up and simply walked away."

"Will you hurry up? The water is drying and we'll have no trail at all." Mabel had no patience.

Against his better judgment, Tucker shrugged his shoulders and followed her though the garden room and patio. "Wild goose chase," he muttered.

"Yesterday there were three lawn chairs in the water and Gevano practically accused Ruthie Sue of throwing them in. Now, look, the trail gives out at the grass but it should show up just beyond in the woods."

"*If* there was a body. *If* it was dragged away. I'll follow you, Miss Marple, but this had better be on the level."

Mabel paused to stare at him, her eyebrows hiked in a quizzical expression.

"Agatha Christie's amateur sleuth," he explained. "Jane Marple."

"Oh, well, then I suppose I'm in good company."

At the beginning of the woods, Mabel discovered bushes bent and broken as though something fairly heavy had been dragged through them. Small beads of water, like dirty mercury, rolled around on the dry ground when Tucker touched them with his toe. They followed the fairly obvious trail into the woods. The trees were mostly hardwood: oaks, sassafras and poplar. A few pines dotted the woods. This area only extended 30 yards or so and beyond it was a tobacco field. A narrow work road led from the field and into the woods. Mabel was having trouble with the uneven terrain.

"Perhaps we had better go back," Tucker said.

"And give up? That's not my way." Mabel believed that Tucker was usually a fair and reasonable man, and when he picked up a dirty damp sneaker, her heart skipped a beat.

He turned the shoe over and poured water from it. "Something awful and strange is going on," he whispered.

"See? I told you!" Miss Marple urged him on. "There is a body and all we have to do is find him."

"Yeah. Find him." Tucker scratched his head.

"Look!" Mabel whispered and pointed to their right. They could see an old tobacco barn, with a rusty tin roof. About half the roof had been blown away. Next to the barn was a Ford truck that looked as old as Mabel felt. "Do you think anyone is still there?" she asked, losing some of her bravado.

"You stay here and I will check," Tucker told her.

"No, I'm coming with you." She was as determined as a hen trying to protect her chicks, and she wasn't about to let him leave her alone.

Tucker sighed. "Listen to me. We are not two Hollywood actors in a heart-wrenching murder mystery!" More gently he added, "Let me look around and I'll signal, then you can come."

"Yes, Doctor," she said meekly. She supposed there was nothing wrong with waiting that long. She watched him saunter down the path toward the old truck. There was a bit of caution in his stance. *It is remarkable that he came to help me. How many other men would have responded to my incomprehensible request? He must think I am a nut and a pest.* She watched him search the property and then he waved to Mabel.

They stood at the back of the truck and studied the brown canvas tarp thrown across it. "Lift the tarp," Mabel suggested.

"No. I'm going back for the police."

Mabel scrunched up her eyes and mouth and made a face at him. "Oh, don't be a nincompoop. If you won't lift it, help me up into the truck and I'll see what's under it."

"Honestly, Mabel, sometimes you exasperate me to death." He pulled up the edge of the tarp and they could see a sneaker that matched the one Tucker had found. They could see, also, worn and faded blue jeans.

"Good Lord," Tucker said.

"Yes, dear Lord, please help us with the body." And to Tucker, she added, "I don't like to hear people misusing the Lord's name."

If she thought Tucker would drop his head in shame, he disappointed her. He was suddenly convulsed with laughter. Mabel's brow twisted in a frown. He couldn't seem to control the spasms that ripped through his chest. "Well, the Good Lord did help us find the 'body,'" he said between guffaws. "As my lawyer friend would say, now we have the *corpus delicti.*" He reached into the bed of the truck and yanked on one of the "legs". He brought out the other sneaker and a handful of pine straw. "Your 'body' is a scarecrow."

Perhaps it was relief, but Mabel's spirit folded inward. "You are not going to faint on me, are you?" Tucker asked. She could hear the alarm in his voice.

Her voice was barely audible. "I see a clue." Her mind was working on something else. She was beginning to remember where she had seen Manuel's helper before.

"Clue?"

"Yes. That red cap in the truck belongs to the gardener, Manuel's helper, Lennie."

Tucker's eyes widened and he seemed to be studying her with awe. "You have some spunk, Mabel Yancey!"

She felt so tired she wasn't sure she could walk home. Her leg hurt terribly. Tucker had ignored her walking trouble.

"Perhaps I had better stay here to see that no one moves the truck and you go back to get the authorities," she suggested.

"No one will get the truck. Now, you just rest a minute." Without warning, he picked her up and set her on the tail gate of the truck. "You don't weigh much more than the bags of sunflower seeds I buy to feed the birds," he said with a chuckle.

The lift to the tailgate was sudden and unexpected but brought immediate relief to her aching limbs. She rubbed her knee; she dreaded the journey home.

Tucker hurried to the front of the truck and raised the creaky hood. He fumbled around a bit and slammed the hood down and rejoined Mabel. "The truck is going nowhere. It is disabled."

"What did you do?" she gasped, her eyes wide with admiration.

"I disconnected the coil wire." When he reached around her to lift her down, she had a great desire to put her arms around his neck and kiss his cheek, but she kept control of unbecoming and possibly unwanted impulses.

"Tucker, you are the most ingenious and the most magnanimous man alive."

With that sentence she made up for all the early morning nuisance she had caused him. He tucked a dripping sneaker into each hip pocket. He grinned down at her. "Okay, Miss Marple, let's go. Here, take my arm." He heard her sigh and he tucked her thin arm under his. He stood up a bit straighter. *I wish my Dorrie could have known Mabel. They would get along famously.* "Watch out for that sassafras root," he advised gently.

Mabel paused a minute. "You know, we did some pretty good work."

He chuckled. "Yep! Especially for old codgers!"

Chapter Ten

When they came to the edge of the woods, they could see that the parking lot was filled with patrol cars, an ambulance and even a fire truck.

"Uh, oh," Tucker said. Blue and amber lights were flashing, making it look like a gaudy Christmas setting. "My intentions were to maintain a low profile with the police and sheriff's department."

"Why on earth would you say that, Tucker?"

"I can't tell," he replied mysteriously. "You just have to trust me."

She gave him an inquiring glance but he seemed deadly serious. "Poor Ruthie Sue," Mabel said. "Let's hurry!"

"Is 'hurry' the only word you know?"

"What better word?" she asked.

"How about 'coffee' and 'breakfast'?"

They went across the patio and through the garden room. As they entered, Ruthie Sue let out a screech that hurt their ears. "There they are! Ask them!"

Ruthie Sue sat in a lawn chair with paramedics and police officers surrounding her. To her right knelt Mrs. Devereux, the director. To her left, Nurse Mary held her hand taking her pulse. Gevano left the group and was rolling a wheel chair toward Tucker and Mabel.

"Here, Miss Mabel. Have a seat."

"Thank you, Gevano. I don't mind if I do." She sank into it, dropping her cane, which Tucker and Gevano bumped heads over trying to retrieve.

A police officer stepped toward them. Tucker reached behind his back and took the wet sneakers from his pockets. "Evidence," he said, as he extended them to the officer.

"Evidence? What evidence?" Captain Patterson wanted to know.

Mabel spoke before Tucker did. "Why from the body, of course."

"What body?" The officer was getting agitated.

Tucker was getting impatient. "The body that had been in the pool. It's out there in the woods in an old truck. As I pointed out, the sneakers are evidence."

Captain Patterson put his hands at his waist like an angry schoolmarm. He glared at them. "You found a crime scene and you damaged evidence? Did you contaminate anything else?"

"Just the truck." Mabel beamed at Tucker.

"The truck? You contaminated the crime scene?" He almost jumped on them.

"Tucker just disabled it so it couldn't be moved. We didn't touch the red cap that belongs to Manuel's helper." She lifted her shoulders and pushed out her chest like a proud peacock.

"I'll have to get a statement from each of you." The officer was not happy.

"First, kind sir," Tucker said, and he was already moving toward the door. "I'm going to go across the street to the convenience store and grab myself a cup of coffee."

"Go with him, sergeant." The officer pointed to one

of his men. "He might want to go to his apartment and change clothes. His rear end is wet."

When Tucker left, followed by the policeman, the captain said, "The rest of you guys go search the woods. Better take the paramedics with you." To Mabel he said: "Okay, start from the beginning. What did you see?"

"What did Ruthie Sue tell you?" Mabel put a finger to her mouth and frowned, hedging for time. She wished Tucker had stayed. He was better about this than she was.

Captain Patterson sputtered. "I want to know what you saw."

Mabel bristled. "You are very abrasive. Did you know that? I am perfectly willing to cooperate."

He backed away and with theatrical courtesy, bowed, and began again. "Mrs. Yancey, please tell me what you saw when you came in here this morning, if you do not mind."

Well, thought Mabel, *If he is going to be that way, I'll have a little fun.* "Ruthie Sue and I saw a man—well, actually, he could have been a boy, or I suppose it could have been a girl—dressed in faded blue jeans and a checkered shirt, floating, face down in the far end of the pool. Oh, yes, he was wearing sneakers."

Captain Patterson rolled his eyes. "Did you touch anything?"

Mabel was a bit huffy. "Well, yes. I grabbed Ruthie Sue's towel and tried to help her as she got sick and threw up. She is very sensitive and frightens easily. She was as white as a sheet and throwing up. I took her into the bathroom to help her clean up. You may be able to locate some of that 'evidence,' over there." She pointed to a spot on the apron of the pool.

"Did you call the police, Mrs. Yancey?"

"No, sir." She looked at him blankly.

"Did you call 911?"

"No, sir," she replied innocently.

"Did you call security?" He was clearly losing his cool again.

Mabel explained, "When we came out of the bathroom, the body was gone. I called Tucker—Dr. Tucker Quick."

"Why, may I ask, did you call Dr. Quick?"

Mabel stared at him. "Don't get so grouchy, young man. I told you I would cooperate! I called Tucker because I knew he would help me find out what was going on."

Captain Patterson sighed. "Is Dr. Quick trained in investigative police work?"

"I have no idea." Mabel smoothed down her blouse. "I did know that he would help me because he is the helping kind."

"Okay. Okay. So why did you and Dr. Quick go into the woods?"

"To find the body, of course. That should be obvious."

Captain Patterson held up his hands and turned around in a complete circle. Mabel could see the frustration building again. She stood up and limped to the far end of the pool with him following.

"It's dry now, but see where I am pointing? There was water here and it made a trail that we could follow." She noticed pine straw in the pool for the first time. "This way." She led them to the patio door. Gevano followed with the wheel chair.

"You keep saying the 'body'. How can you be so sure

the victim was dead?"

Suddenly Mabel's face lit up and with a twinkle in her eye she said, "He was not alive." And with that, she sank into the chair Gevano was holding behind her.

Before the interrogation could continue, the other policemen and the paramedics entered the garden room. On a gurney, they carried "the body."

Patterson's mouth fell open. "Do you mean we have wasted all this time on a straw-stuffed dummy?"

"No!" Mabel said, "We have investigated why someone is trying to scare Ruthie Sue to death. I know who it is and I know why."

"Who?" Gevano asked.

"Yes," the captain said, "who and why?" They had moved back to Ruthie Sue and the others.

"I, also, would very much like to know," Dev said.

Mabel told her, "I think it's Lennie."

"Lennie? Manuel's new helper?" Dev looked flabbergasted. She didn't lose any time, however, in pushing numbers on her cell phone. "Get Manuel and Lennie to the pool now," she barked.

When they arrived, she asked Manuel how well he knew his assistant.

"I don't know 'til he come to work," the gardener insisted.

Tucker, trailed by the policeman, returned and Mabel noted that he was much better dressed and looked far more intelligent with dry pants and a shirt on, rather than his pajama tops. He wore bright red suspenders. Captain Patterson gazed at him with a little more respect.

To Lennie, the captain said, "What are you trying to do by scaring two old women to death?"

"I didn't try nothing. I wasn't scaring two old women."

Captain Patterson put his hands at his waist. "What do you call it, then?"

Lennie whined. "I don't call it nothing."

"Well, you did. You have terrorized these two frail old ladies. Look, kid, we found evidence. See these blue jeans? We know this is your cap."

"So what?" He sneered at Ruthie Sue and she shrank back against the chair.

"We also found your truck—registered to your father and fingerprints are everywhere. My officers are checking them now—but I believe we will find they are yours." The captain spoke sternly.

Lennie pouted. "This woman," he pointed to Ruthie Sue, "she out to get my brother."

Mabel interrupted. "Doesn't Lennie remind you of anyone, Ruthie Sue?"

"I don't know. Who?"

"I went to the trial with you. When your car was hijacked at WalMart," Mabel explained to her.

Ruthie Sue pointed to Lennie. "He didn't take my car."

Mabel sighed impatiently. "No. But, his brother did. At knife point."

"That's right, officer." Ruthie Sue continued, "I thought he reminded me of someone. It was his brother."

Mabel told him, "Captain, this man's brother hijacked Ruthie Sue's car and she testified against him and he went to jail."

Captain Patterson clapped his hands together. "A light begins to dawn." He said, "I remember now." He turned to Lennie. "So, you tried to scare two old women because your brother stole a car from one of them."

Lennie protested, "He wasn't going to steal it. Just take it for a short ride."

"Yeah," the captain said, "took it with a knife at her throat. Wrecked it. Totaled it, I remember."

"You can't arrest me." Lennie was whining again.

"Really? Can we arrest him, sergeant?"

"Yes, sir, I believe we can. Turn around, sonny boy." He put handcuffs on Lennie.

Captain Patterson reminded him, "Read him his Miranda Rights. And if you don't cooperate, young man, we'll add resisting arrest charges. Take him in and book him for malicious mischief. Look at the mess you made in this pool," he held up a handful of pine straw, "to say nothing of the pain you caused these poor old women."

"They ain't poor," Lennie said.

"Oh, they ain't—rather—are not poor? Does that give you the right to torture them?"

"I didn't do nothing to them."

"Nothing, except trying to drive Ruthie Sue crazy," Tucker interjected.

"Ain't too swift, anyway," muttered Lennie.

"That's enough!" Mrs. Devereux said. "Take him away, officer!"

ഇര

Ruthie Sue lagged behind Mabel and Tucker as they walked back to their building. When they slowed up, she slowed up. Finally, Mabel shrugged her shoulders and continued at her normal rate—which was not particularly fast.

"Well, Miss Marple, what are you going to do for an encore?" Tucker asked.

"I have resigned as your fictional sleuth. Tomorrow

I'm going to lunch with Charlene."

"Wait," Ruthie Sue suddenly called out. "I didn't thank you, Tucker and Mabel."

Tucker rolled his eyes before he turned to face her. "I wouldn't have missed the adventure for anything. You are very welcome."

"And you, Tucker Quick, had better have a little talk with your God and ask Him to forgive you for your lying," Mabel said quietly.

"Why, Mabel Yancey. What are you talking about?"

"Huh?" Ruthie Sue asked.

"Nothing." Mabel replied.

Chapter Eleven

It was a sunlit spring morning when Charlene drove her mother with her new neighbor, Grace Guimares and her daughter, Katlin, to Raleigh for lunch. Their window table at The Rose Bud Tea Room gave them a view of a garden draped with lavender wisteria and a display of yellow and red tulips. Their table had a bouquet of pink rosebuds that accented the pink tablecloth and napkins. The fragrance of exotic teas permeated the room.

Charlene had brought her mother here before but this was the first chance she had to spend time with Grace and Katlin. She wondered if they could measure up to the praise her mother had for them.

Grace was one of the prettiest ladies Charlene had ever seen. Her white hair was perfectly cut and styled and her large blue eyes gave her an incredibly youthful look. Mabel had wrinkles—much to her displeasure—but Grace's skin was firm and smooth. She was intelligent and pleasant—just the kind of friend her mother needed. Perhaps she could balance out the time Mabel spent with Ruthie Sue. Katlin was also extremely attractive and personable. Charlene was pleased.

After they gave their orders, Mabel asked Grace, "Did you know that Noah Malone is a fine pianist?"

Grace wrinkled her brow. "Noah Malone? Is he that

quiet man who sits in the back of the room when we have Bible Study?"

"Yes. He was a real estate agent in Watauga County and also worked as an accompanist in the music department at Appalachian State University."

"Have you heard him play?" Katlin asked.

Mabel shook out her napkin and placed it on her lap. "Not since he has moved here. There's really no place for him to practice—except the auditorium where there is no privacy."

Charlene said, "I heard him in a concert in Boone and he gave a tremendous concert. I didn't realize that he was a resident at Dogwood Glenn."

Mabel said, "He's been here for about six months. He moved in shortly before you did, Grace."

Grace worked silently with her napkin. She kept her eyes on her hands until Katlin suggested, "Mom, let him play your piano. He sounds like a professional."

Grace's voice sounded defensive to Charlene. "Oh, I don't know. I hardly know the man." She seemed greatly distressed to Charlene. Mabel and Katlin exchanged glances and Charlene wondered what was going on.

No one spoke for a moment. Watching her mother, Charlene was surprised how quickly she changed the conversation. "Have you made any predictions on the NCAA Championship?" Mabel asked.

Charlene said, "Mother loves sports. She keeps her TV on the sports channel and her radio on the classical music station. Often simultaneously."

Everyone laughed and the tension was broken. Katlin said, "I can just see Tyler Hansbrough dribbling the ball to a Vienna Waltz!"

Grace laughed and began to tilt her shoulders to the right and then to the left as though in dance. "One-two-three. One-two-three." She was joined by the other three.

"One-two-three." Grace hummed *The Blue Danube.*

The waitress, bringing their spinach salads, put down the tray at the next table and she began to sway as though she heard the music also. "One-two-three."

After their fun, Katlin said, "Mabel, can I ask you a personal question?"

"Well, I have been quite personal with my questions. Why not?"

"I rarely see you when you are not wearing purple or lavender. Is there a special reason, or do you just like purple?" Katlin asked.

Mabel smiled. "I do like purple, and that is the color I wore in my wedding to Will Yancey. Wearing purple always keeps me feeling a little closer to my Will."

Katlin reached over to touch Mabel's hand. "That's a beautiful thought."

Mabel explained, "We all grieve and remember in our own way."

Charlene reached over to pat her mother's hand and she noticed Katlin putting an arm around her mother's shoulders.

ꕥ

Mabel was on the deck watering her flowers when she looked down to street level and saw Noah Malone approaching Bougainvillea Hall. She had been wanting to talk with him so she put down her watering can and hurried to the fourth floor lobby. She arranged a chair so she could watch the elevator. She prayed, "Lord, don't let me mess this up. He's a bit skittish."

She heard the "ping" of the elevator. "Noah. Rev. Malone," she called to him, as he stepped out. He looked younger than most of the other men in the building.

He turned to face her. "Mabel? Are you addressing me?" He looked startled. *No,* she decided. *He looks stricken. Oh, goodness, what am I doing?*

As he approached her, she said, "I think you are the one to teach our Bible Study."

He stared at her. Opened his mouth, then pressed his lips together tightly. He stood silently looking at his shoes as Mabel watched him. "I thought I had achieved anonymity here," he said sadly. He took a deep breath.

"Why, Noah, why would you need to be anonymous? Please, come sit down."

He pulled a chair up close to her. "If you know who I am, you know that I have no right to teach a Bible Study."

"I do know who you are and you have every right. Noah, we lived in Boone for many years and two of our best friends were Dr. and Mrs. Allan Watson—who, as you know, pastored near there for years."

"You knew Betty and Allan?" He was clearly baffled.

"I know that you are eminently qualified to lead our study. I talked with Betty this morning."

"Oh, what a dear Betty is. How is she?" he asked.

"She sends you her love. She told me she could not break any confidences but that you were not to blame for your wife's death. I had read about the accident in the paper and thought that was who you were, but I don't know any details."

"I'm flabbergasted. I haven't served as a minister since my wife died. If I hadn't reported my car stolen, she and her friend might still be alive." He dropped his forehead and covered his face with his hands.

Mabel put her hand on his shoulder. "I have no right nor the necessary skills to give you counsel, but I know that Allan did. Betty told me that your wife had run away before and that you took her back—like Hosea in the Bible. We need you. Will you consider it and pray about it? I have done it for years and I'm so weary." She sighed and rubbed her shoulder as though it was giving her terrible pain. She realized she was putting on quite an act.

"But, Mabel—do you have bursitis? I'm so sorry. I'll pray about this but the others may not accept me." He pulled his argyle sweater closer and began to button it.

"Why wouldn't they accept you? Do you think the rest of us are perfect?"

"Oh, yes," he said seriously and they laughed together.

Mabel said quietly, "Get out your Bible and go to work."

"Hey, hold on," Noah said. "I said I would *think* about it."

"You said you would *pray* about it."

Noah smiled. "Mabel, I don't know what to think about you."

"I confuse lots of people."

"Will I need to … to … explain things?" he asked as he stood up.

"That is totally up to you. You owe no one an explanation. I'll let you tell your story in any way you want to but, you tell it only if you want to when you want to."

He hugged her. "Thank you, Mabel, for believing in me. Since Allan Watson died, I've never had another close friend."

"God bless you and use you, dear man."

Chapter Twelve

Mabel was enjoying a wonderful sleep when the phone blasted her awake. As always, her first thought was that there was an emergency in the family. She glanced at the clock and saw that it was 12:05 a.m. She said aloud, "If that is you, Ruthie Sue, I'm going to strangle you."

She pulled the phone to her ear. "Ma-Ma-Mabel," someone stuttered. "Mabel, I'm frightened to death."

"Etta Worthington, if you are frightened, call security."

"I'm too scared, and I don't know the number." Etta confessed.

Mabel pulled herself up and leaned on her elbow. Etta lived on the 1st floor of her building. "You are supposed to keep the number taped to your phone. What happened?"

Etta had caused quite a scene after the tornado when Dolly's dog found shelter under her skirt.

"I left my draperies open so I could watch the sunset." Etta explained, "Then, I put on my gown to watch TV. When I got up to turn the TV off someone from outside whistled at me. It frightened the living daylights out of me. Mabel? Mabel?"

Mabel was exasperated. "Someone whistled at you?"

"Yes. It was, you know, a fox whistle. *Wheet Whew!*"

Mabel was fully awake now and laughing. "You mean it was a *wolf* whistle."

"It came from right outside my window," Etta said. "Why is this funny?"

"Well, Etta, you and I are not exactly whistle bait."

Etta's voice rose a whole octave. "Women our age are getting raped every day. And I was Miss Squash Blossom in 1936. For North Carolina."

"Why did you call me?" Mabel asked. "My apartment is a mile away from you."

"You can scare them off."

"I can? Why does everybody believe I can solve all the problems? What do you think we pay security for? I'm not coming down four floors to scare your fox away. And I wasn't even runner up for Miss North Carolina Squash Blossom."

Mabel could imagine the rotund Etta shivering in her flannel night gown. She began to snicker again. "Did you scream?"

"Well, that's a stupid question. Of course, I screamed."

"Then," Mabel said, "your fox is miles away. Etta, close your drapes and go to bed. Or, you can call Todd. Dolly's Chihuahua, Baby, is a fine watchdog."

"You are making fun of me, Mabel."

"Yes, I am and I'm sorry. I'll call security for you but you'll have to stay up to answer the night watchman's questions."

"Okay. When will he come?"

"I don't know, Etta, but I want to go back to bed. Okay?"

"Okay. You are the one who always knows what to do."

For crying out-loud, Mabel thought as she called security and then she lay awake for a long time. She had been unkind. *Poor Etta.* She was still hoping her Prince Charming would come sweep her off her feet. Etta had told her about her childhood and growing up with a cruel, dictatorial father. "He was as mean as a snake and chased any prospective suitors away."

Apparently the old man had made her existence miserable, never allowing her to go to college, work or marry. The one time she defied him was when she secretly entered the beauty pageant. Her father made life a living hell for her after her mother died. She said he was so mean that she assumed she would have to hire pall bearers for his funeral. But by the time the old man went on to his reward—or lack of it—all his contemporaries, and most of their sons were gone. Men who didn't know him well didn't hesitate to carry the casket for his last stroll.

But, the old man left her a "ton of money" since she was the only heir. She had been too timid to travel and she had been so satiated in frugal living that she found no pleasure in spending money. After he died, she spent her time as a volunteer in the church kindergarten.

Poor Etta. Mabel sighed. She had been blessed with two marriages and several more proposals. Now she thanked the Lord for all He had given to her. "Now, Dear Lord, please bring some happiness to Etta!"

ꕥ

Two days later, Mabel was surprised to hear from her hairdresser, Raymie, that Etta had a secret admirer. Why hadn't Etta told Mabel herself?

"She found this beautiful card in her mailbox just before she came by here," Raymie explained. "I'm going to perm her this afternoon and you know how forgetful she is. She needed to check again on the time."

"Does she have any idea who sent the card?"

"She thinks it might be Dr. Quick because she saw him near her box just before the card was discovered."

Mabel said, quickly, "Oh, I hardly think so. Dr. Quick is still very much in love with his wife. He is still grieving her death. He is not yet ready for another relationship." Mabel felt weak behind the knees and a strange, sick feeling hit her in the pit of her stomach.

Raymie expressed concern. "Mabel, are you all right? You are as white as a sheet."

What on earth is wrong with me, Mabel wondered. *Surely I couldn't be jealous. Of Etta? And Tucker? Nonsense.*

To Raymie, she said, "I hope no one is playing a joke on Etta. That would be cruel."

"Perhaps she does have an admirer. There are women less attractive here," Raymie said.

Mabel leaned over and peered in the mirror. "Age has now stamped with its signet that ingenuous brow." Again, she quoted a poet whose name she couldn't remember. She rubbed her finger across the wide wrinkle.

"Now you are quoting some poet I never heard of," Raymie said. "You're brilliant."

"No, I don't even know the poet's name. When you grow older, you don't grow wiser; you merely hide your ignorance better," Mabel said "Why don't you get some fancy wrinkle cream to sell in here. You would make a fortune. Even my grandson told me the other day that all very old ladies have wrinkles."

Raymie said, "I saw an ad for a cream that says it fights

wrinkles and helps skin defy gravity. I'll look into it."

"And while you are at it, get a stock on the gardenia perfume you usually wear. I really enjoy it. I notice you are not using it today."

"I need something stronger because Etta is coming back." Raymie began to laugh again. "What I mean is that I needed something to combat the aroma of the perm chemicals. This is called Eternal Peony, but it might make Bette sneeze when she comes to work."

"Do you know that sweet little Janet? She told me that Bob is finally paying more attention to her since she found a perfume that smells like eBay!" Mabel was doing her best to feel more cheerful.

Chapter Thirteen

Tucker Quick moved like a man with a mission, on his way to an important appointment. Years in the academic and administrative posts at the university, plus a natural shyness made him appear to be preoccupied. This behavior insulated him from petty gossip and maudlin conversations. This evening he was in a hurry to get to the pharmacy before dinner.

"Tucker! Dr. Quick!"

Tucker turned back toward his apartment building. "Oh, hello, Marylouise. Hello, Etta. How are you both doing?" He might have escaped but they stepped to either side of him and Marylouise laid her hand on his arm.

"I have been meaning to talk with you, Tucker," Marylouise said. "I'm going to start an art class and I thought you might be interested. Etta is going to be in it."

Etta gave him an enthusiastic grin. "Come on. It will be fun."

He didn't want to be rude, he just had other transactions on his mind. "No, thanks. I'm really no good—" When he saw that Marylouise was going to object, he added, "I'm really not interested. My HAM radio and books keep me busy."

"Please. Just think about it," Etta pled.

"I just did. My answer remains no."

They looked so dejected that he offered a consolation prize. "I'll tell you what I will do, Marylouise. If you'll paint a picture of that bunch of old men, who meet each evening under the dogwood tree to settle all the world's problems, I'll buy it. It's an informal discussion group led by Matt. You can make it like a Norman Rockwell painting." He freed his arm from Marylouise and hurried down the sidewalk. He shouldn't have been impolite, but he just panicked, he told himself.

Mabel was already in the dining room and he walked to her table just as he saw Etta move to it. He hesitated, but Mabel was beckoning him on. He usually sat with her and often they were joined by the doctors Sam and Stella and Grace Guimares. He looked forward each evening to lively, friendly conversations.

He was a bit surprised to see Etta in a dressy apricot silk blouse and skirt to match move to the seat next to Mabel. She wobbled on high heels. She reminded him of a sweet potato on stilts.

When she sat down, Mabel said, "Etta, you have a new hairdo."

"How do you like it, Tucker?" She fluttered her eyelashes at him.

"Like what?" Tucker asked.

"My new hairdo. I got a permanent and color. Champagne Blond."

"Very nice."

She gave him a million dollar smile. "I'm so glad you like it."

What is wrong with that woman today? What did it matter if he liked her hair or, for that matter, that she was going to take an art class? He decided it was time to go to the salad bar, but as he stood up to get a salad plate, Etta joined him. He suddenly lost his appetite. "What is wrong with that woman?" he whispered to Mabel when he returned to his seat.

"You should know," Mabel replied. He noticed some glee in her voice.

"What do you mean, I should know?" He forgot to whisper.

"Know what?" Etta asked as she returned with her salad.

"We were commenting on your lipstick and earrings, Etta," Mabel said.

Tucker understood how much Mabel liked to needle him but tonight he was sure he looked confused enough to be pathetic, even in her eyes. She took pity on him and leaned toward him to whisper, "I'll tell you later."

No one had ever been more welcome to their table than Dr. Sam was when he slipped into the seat next to Tucker. Dr. Stella and Grace Guimares took up the other places. Noah had been joining them lately but tonight he had been replaced by Etta.

Tucker concentrated on a debate with Sam about the problems of Medicare. He did however, overhear Mabel tell Etta that Willie Dewitt was smiling at her. "He seems to find you unusually attractive tonight."

"Willie? He is so uncouth," was Etta's response.

"What do you mean by uncouth?" Tucker couldn't resist asking.

"Just listen to his loud belly laugh," Etta explained.

"I like a man with a hearty laugh. Shows he has a zest for life!" Tucker said.

He saw that Mabel continued to watch Willie and when Etta dropped her napkin, Mabel nodded to him. Willie nearly knocked his table over getting up and then almost lost his balance as he retrieved the napkin. "Here you are, pretty lady."

Etta looked startled and her face turned a shade pinker than her lipstick. She murmured a thank you but didn't look at Willie. He returned to his table, flushed and self-conscious.

"Willie is quite the gentleman," Sam said, just as their entrees were delivered. Stella and Grace agreed quietly.

ꙮ

Tucker was usually in a hurry to get home to watch the news, but tonight he left the table as quickly as it was graceful to do so, and deviated from his usual custom. He wanted no further contact with Etta until he knew what was happening. He made a dash for the pink dogwood tree. Matt was already there, positioning his wheel chair so he could enlist others into his discussion group. Matt—much younger than any other resident—came to Dogwood Glenn with his parents. He had been in a wheelchair all his life but was remarkably free from bitterness. He had an alert mind and was a favorite among the other "Glenners" as he called the residents.

"I see it's time for your discussion group, Matt. Would you like to have someone new to grumble with?" Tucker asked.

Matt's laughter rang out across the campus. It was joyful and energetic and lifted Tucker's spirits. "What's the matter? You fleeing from one of us?"

"Why would you say that?" Tucker asked quickly, hoping he was not blushing.

"Well, I see you walking home with one each night and I saw both Marylouise and Etta hanging on you as you were leaving. to go to dinner," Matt said. "Would you like to help solve the world's problems with us? We'd be honored to have you join us, Tucker. Here comes Oscar."

"I'll listen tonight, Matt. See if I have enough brain power to keep up with you," Tucker said. "As a man grows older, he either talks more and says less or talks less and says more."

Lewis arrived. "I'm good at solving the world's problems." He scratched his head. "Tell me, do I come here often?" His inane remark brought the usual snickers.

"Apparently you are not good enough. The world still has its problems," Oscar said.

"Time to call this meeting to order. Good, here is Chandler. The court is in session."

Chandler meandered over slowly, due to a recent knee injury. He took his place on the bench. "Growing old is the pits. Just when you start getting forgetful, the doctor prescribes dozens of pills that you have to remember to take."

"Wait a minute," Tucker said. "We are old. Since we are old and revered, we should be wise."

Chandler reminded them of the old adage, "Age carries all things away—even the mind."

Laughter rumbled across the walkway. Matt said, "I have a solution. Let's just not get old."

Tucker couldn't resist. "Easy for you to say. Why Matt, you are just a boy. You are still wet behind the ears!" He looked around to make sure that Etta and the others from the dining room were gone and then he said goodbye to the group of men and walked to this apartment.

Chapter Fourteen

Mabel had been waiting for Tucker and as soon as he approached the door, she jerked it open. "Shhhh," she warned. "Come hear something beautiful!"

She took hold of his red suspenders and propelled him toward the deck. They stood by the open door and listened to piano music—resonant and melodic.

"Grace?" Tucker asked.

"No, it's Noah playing her piano. He told me he had found some duet music and was going to show it to her tonight. He is trying to entice her to play with him."

"Noah plays wonderfully!" Tucker acknowledged. "A real pro. Have you heard Grace yet?"

"Only for a minute or two. But, Noah is going to get her to play." Mabel was convinced.

There was a pause in the music, then another touch—a lighter one, a tentative chord and a few faltering runs. Gradually, the hesitation disappeared and they were certain Grace was at the keyboard. In a minute or two, they could tell a duet was in progress.

Tucker grinned. "You are behind this. Are you some kind of a miracle worker?"

"Proof's in the pudding. I'm just a meddling old fool. I just knew if I could get two musicians together, there would be a positive result." Mabel pulled the sliding door closed, explaining that it was getting a bit chilly.

Tucker sat down on the couch and took the bull by the horns. "I won't deny that you are meddling; but you're no fool. Okay, Mabel, explain."

Her eyes danced with merriment. "Explain what?"

"You know perfectly well what I mean. What was going on with Etta Worthington and is she going to continue to stalk me?"

Mabel slapped his shoulder. "Oh, hush, Tucker. Etta thought you were the gentleman who sent her a secret admirer card." She eased into her blue leather chair across from him.

"What?" There was no humor in his response. As he knew she would, Mabel expressed pleasure at his consternation.

"She saw you near her box just before she discovered the card and assumed you were the sender."

"Of all the asinine, featherbrained, idiotic ideas I ever heard. Didn't you tell her I didn't send it?" he demanded.

"How was I supposed to know that you had not sent it?" she asked demurely.

"You are not completely mindless. How could you be that absurd?"

"Oh, it's pretty easy. When you have preposterous friends you tend to get a little wacky also." She was laughing. "I heard the card was sappy."

"What does that mean? Well, it wasn't me," he said emphatically.

"Don't shout, Tucker. I didn't think it was you. I just hope no one is playing a joke on her. Yesterday was April Fool's Day."

Tucker rubbed his jaw. "Poor old woman. I'll bet it

was Willie. He has little enough sense."

"I think it was Willie, also. I hope he wasn't just teasing her. Can you talk with him, Tucker?"

"I positively will not. I'm staying completely clear of any bizarre plan you devise."

Mabel persisted, "But, what if she gets hurt?"

"Why is that my problem?"

"Because, you are so kind-hearted." Mabel looked at him coyly.

"I'm not crazy! Just leave them alone, for crying out loud. They are both adults."

Mabel nodded in ready agreement.

Tucker felt uncomfortable. Mabel, he knew, seldom left things to simmer and her mind was already dizzily spinning possibilities. He threw up his hands in defeat. "I'm going home."

"I baked a cake …"

"I don't care if you made banana pudding. I'm tired and I'm going home." He, however, had his hand on the door knob when he paused. "What would you think if you found a secret admirer card in your box?"

Possibly, she would ignore him. But he heard a soft reply, "I'd hope it was from you, Tucker."

Gently, he pulled the door closed. *That's like something my Dorrie would say.*

He wasn't sure if that knowledge made him uneasy or pleased.

Chapter Fifteen

Rachelle Moffitt lived on the 1st floor of Mabel's building and was not a regular visitor to Mabel's apartment, so when she came to the door and called softly, "May I come in?" Mabel was surprised. Rachelle had appeared reserved and standoffish, but Mabel had been fascinated by her career in opera and stage.

"Why, dear, how lovely you look!" Mabel pushed the remote to turn off the golf tournament. "You have so many beautiful clothes."

Rachelle said. "I have too many clothes. I haven't unpacked all the boxes of formal wear I brought." She wore a long sleeved silk blouse in the softest of yellow, exactly the color of her hair, and a full paisley-printed skirt. It looked to Mabel like she wore a half dozen petticoats. She had on a wide brown belt and brown high heels. "I brought you something. You do have a CD player, don't you?"

"Of course I have a CD player and a DVD player and a dozen other apparatuses that I hardly know how to use—much to the displeasure of my grandkids."

"Would you like to have this? My agent found a box of old tapes and had them made into CDs. Some are at the Metropolitan Opera, but this one is at the New York City Opera. *La Traviata*." Rachelle said with matter-of-fact ease.

"Oh, Rachelle. I've never been to a real opera. Tucker will love this also." Mabel took the CD and gently inserted it into her Bose player.

"You don't have to listen to it now! I've heard it." She laughed.

"Of course I want to hear it now!" Mabel insisted.

"It's old—1950s. Beverly Sills sang the lead, Violetta. I don't play the most important part of course, but you can hear me. I sang the part of the maid, Annina."

"Splendid," Mabel said and when the music burst forth, she dialed Tucker. "Come hear what I have!" The three sat silently, listening to several renditions on the CD. Tucker commented, "Dorrie and I saw *La Traviata* in New York and also in Milan. Beverly Sills was effervescent."

Tucker asked her when she sang in New York. "We might have heard you!"

Rachelle blushed with embarrassment. "I hope I did not represent myself as a star. I sang the part a few times in New York, but never in Milan," she said modestly. "Most of my work at the New York City Opera was in the late '50's."

"Well, I am delighted to hear you now! We didn't visit New York until much later."

For several moments, the only sound came from the Bose. Tucker said, quietly, "I had no idea you were a mezzo-soprano! What a magnificent voice!"

Mabel chided her guest. "Why have you never sung for us? We need a recital!"

"Who would accompany me?" She sat regally in a straight chair with her hands folded serenely on her lap. Her full skirt and many petticoats flared out around her.

Mabel marveled at how composed and feminine she looked, and she was at least 75.

Tucker said, "There are two here who could play this accompaniment. Noah Malone or Grace Guimares."

Rachelle looked surprised. "I didn't know they played the piano."

"Those two are professionals, but we have other musicians. If we have a concert, I think we need to ask Gevano to participate." Mabel was getting excited.

Rachelle looked puzzled. "Who's Gevano and what's his music?"

Tucker answered, "He's on the staff and is also pool manager. Fine young man."

"Does he have training?" Rachelle asked, a bit hesitantly.

"I don't know, but he can belt out a few hymns. Tucker, have you heard him sing, "How Great Thou Art?" Anyway, perhaps that's where you come in," Mabel said.

"I don't know any hymns. My training is all classical."

"And your training is a tremendous asset. Perhaps you could give Gevano some lessons," Tucker suggested. "I heard him impersonate Elvis Presley."

Rachelle turned pale. "Elvis Presley? I don't think I have that much time."

"Of course you do. If you just worked with him an evening or two a week, we could have us a wonderful concert," Mabel exclaimed. When Rachelle remained mute, Mabel tried another approach. "What do you know about training canaries?"

"I don't know what you mean, Mabel. What has this to do with canaries?"

"Probably nothing," Mabel conceded. "But there is one on this floor that may be needing a home. Beverly Sills has a beautiful voice."

"Bev is the canary," Tucker said. He frowned and asked, "What's all this about?"

"If Marylouise marries Lloyd Ray, she will have to give away her canary."

Rachelle didn't comment on the bird. Her mind was still on the opera. "Beverly sang Violetta in 300 performances."

"I read her autobiography, *Bubbles*. I would have loved to know her," Mabel said.

"Oh! Yes!" Rachelle clasped her hands in front of her and sat taller on her chair. "She sang with perfection! Her voice was capable of spinning a seemingly endless legato line, or of bursting into waves of dazzling *fioritura* and thrilling high notes."

Rising, Tucker said, "I'll have to take your word for that. I don't understand all those highfalutin words. I need to go. Thanks so much for sharing with me. Your voice took my breath away."

When he was gone, Mabel said, "Dr. and Mrs. Yakamoto are your neighbors, are they not?"

"Yes, they are." Again, Rachelle looked puzzled.

"They are superb teachers. Taught in the Math and Science School. Do you know how they spend their summers? They teach math to disadvantaged children. All summer—in summer camps. It has allowed them to spread their talent and to continue in the field they are so gifted in. Perhaps you, too, have a responsibility to use your talent.

"You have heard that Marylouise, a painter, is teaching an art class. Archie is working with the men's choral group and believe it or not, Arlene Snider is starting a fitness class." Mabel moved to the kitchen and turned on the stove under her tea pot.

"Those people are all much younger than I am," Rachelle said.

"All of them are at least 70 and Archie is approaching 80. I think Dr. Yakamoto is in his early 90's. Their enthusiasm keeps them young. Why don't you just think about it? God has given you a great talent. What kind of tea would you like? I have almond and orange?"

"I love the almond," Rachelle replied.

Mabel poured hot water over the tea and let it brew. "I just thought of several other people here who do great volunteer work. Did you know that Rob Pollard spends each Tuesday at Western Wake Hospital, holding babies in the intensive care nursery?"

"Holding babies? That big, strong, masculine man?"

Mabel carried her prized white tea pot to the coffee table. "Yes! He is highly regarded at the hospital. Evone Herndon volunteers in the Emergency Room."

"But she is a nurse."

"Yes," Mabel agreed, "but retired. Eloise Warfield is a retired teacher and she works two afternoons a week at the elementary school, tutoring. … Sugar and cream?"

They sat for a few minutes sipping their tea, and Mabel noticed that her guest sat with such poise and lifted her cup so daintily that she could have been a guest of Queen Elizabeth. Then Rachelle startled her asking, "What volunteer work do you do?"

"I have taught the young adult Sunday School class in my church for fifty years. And I spend lots of time with Ruthie Sue and others like her who need a bit of tutoring about life."

"I believe that qualifies!" Rachelle said.

Chapter Sixteen

Mabel was not sure she liked the way her children were treating her! Charlene had already invited Tucker and her to Saturday lunch at her home. Charlene said she wanted her family, including dog and cat, to meet Tucker. Now Ed and Sue were having them over. Mabel always loved to visit her children, but clearly they were up to something. Was it to evaluate Tucker? Set her up with him? Surely, they were not playing cupid.

Tucker's daughter Jeanne had them over and Mabel was perfectly comfortable with that visit, but Ed was different. He took the role of a father sometimes, where Mabel was concerned.

Jeeves barked as they pulled into the driveway. Ed had him on the leash when he opened her car door. As usual, Jeeves was a gentleman and greeted Mabel with restraint, but he was obviously thrilled to see her and did not move more than a few feet away from her the entire visit.

Sue had the table set with their finest china and crystal. A bouquet of purple iris was the center piece. Sue knew how much she loved the flowers. Mabel didn't know that Sue had already met Tucker, but she had. From the conversation, Mabel learned that he had visited Ed at his school office at least twice. Why had he not mentioned it to her? She felt a little left out.

The meal was wonderful with baked sea bass in tomato sauce, cole slaw and a tossed green salad. *Perfect,* Mabel thought. The table conversation was light and funny. Ed and Tucker played off each other and each had a wonderful sense of humor.

After lunch, Sue invited Mabel to the back yard to view her flower garden. Mabel loved her daughter-in-law and they shared a common interest in flowers. Mabel admired the garden and was delighted when Sue cut her a large bouquet of pink roses and multi-colored iris. Jeeves remained at her side as they walked around the house to look at other flowers. It reminded Mabel of the time she fell in her own garden.

"Do you remember this variety of jasmine? I started it from a cutting at your house," Sue said.

"I have seen several things that are familiar from my yard. What about that bush of tiny gardenias? Oh, yes, I remember when we cut some. I didn't know you had rooted that also. I am so pleased. You are a dear, Sue! I'm so glad you have such a garden to share with your old mother-in-law! Your garden would be a wonderful spot for a wedding."

"That's romantic. Are you thinking of having a wedding?" Sue sounded a little amused.

"Not for me! Of course not! I was thinking of your children."

When they returned to the house, Tucker and Ed were entrenched in Ed's study and the door was closed. *That's strange,* Mabel thought. *Neither has ever been so secretive that I knew of.*

Sue showed her the latest school pictures of the children, and carefully cut copies for Mabel. "For your grandchildren gallery," Sue said. They talked at length about Sue's work and still the men remained isolated.

"Probably on the HAM," Sue explained, but Mabel thought something more was going on. Each man was working on some mysterious decrypting. Ed had brought Tucker some paperwork from his Army Reserve Unit. "Just to keep you in training," he had explained in front of Mabel.

"Does it not bother you, Sue, that they are working so secretly?"

"I'm used to it. I have my work and my children to keep me busy. I think they might be working on a book. What I don't like is when Ed is called away unexpectedly."

"A book makes sense," Mabel conceded and she felt less anxious. "If we don't leave soon, we will be late for dinner. However, I don't know how we could eat another bite."

The men came out of the study laughing and Tucker reminded Mabel about how bright her son was and told Sue: "What a pleasant time in your home, Sue. You are a wonderful chef and I thank you very much."

On the way home, Mabel was a bit startled when Tucker told her, "Your son asked me if my intentions toward you were honorable. He grilled me on my feelings for you."

Mabel caught her breath. "What did you say?"

"I told him I was an honorable man and that I would marry you if I had to. I saw the shotgun in his study."

Mabel buffed him on the arm. "You did not!"

"What would you want me to say, Mabel?" The car was filled with a palatable expectancy.

"Tucker, I don't want to get married again."

Did he sigh? Mabel thought he did. "First time I was ever turned down before I asked," he said quietly.

"You don't want to get married, either, Tucker."

He waited a full minute to reply and Mabel held her breath. The last thing on earth she wanted to do was to hurt or offend him.

He reached over and took her hand and held it to his cheek. "You are a dear and precious lady. Marriage was a marvelous phase of my life and also of yours. I want to savor the sweet memories of Dorrie these last few years of my life."

They were both quiet for a moment but there was no strain between them now.

"I wouldn't and couldn't take Dorrie's place and I have my Will to remember." Mabel spoke softly. Then she laughed. "I couldn't stand your wandering around the apartment half the night."

"I couldn't stand your going to bed at dark."

Mabel shot back, "I couldn't tolerate your talking on your radio all the time."

"I couldn't put up with all the foolishness you take from Ruthie Sue—or your talking on the phone for hours."

"I think we best live apart, Tucker," she said seriously, "so we don't kill each other."

"But, if I ever do marry again, it would only be to you."

"I adore you, Tucker. You are my best friend. Can we enjoy each other without getting married?"

"And you are my dearest friend, sweet one."

Mabel smiled. "We had better just leave it there."

"Yep! For now."

Chapter Seventeen

Once a month Mabel put on a purple dress, donned a large red hat, and climbed aboard the activities bus to go to lunch with the Glenner Red Hat group. Suzie, the exuberant Activities Director, had unbelievable patience and cheerfully loaded wheel chairs and walkers and took the ladies anywhere in Wake County for a fun meal.

Dogwood Glenn provided one hot meal a day and since most residents choose the evening meal, these Glenners looked forward to the noon day outing. Much creativity went into decorating hats with purple or red flowers and often truckers would grin and wave to them. The average age of this group was 86. Frequently a stranger sitting near them in a restaurant would come talk to them. They always commented about the lovely hats, but also the "spunk" these old ladies showed. Mabel had heard, "I wish my mother—or grandmother—would join the Red Hats" so many times that she thought about carrying copies to give out of the poem by Jenny Joseph that inspired the organization.

"When I am an old woman, I shall wear purple
With a red hat that doesn't go, and doesn't suit me.
And I shall spend my pension on brandy and summer gloves ..."

Today they had reservations at a Japanese restaurant in Crab Apple Mall. Suzie did not enjoy driving on the freeways, so she often took back roads, which pleased the Glenners even more. They enjoyed the opportunity to get a glimpse of the budding spring. The late cold snap did not appear to have done any damage.

Mabel leaned back and closed her eyes. She loved listening to the other women.

Barbara said, "I get sick and tired of my husband referring to our marriage as a 'sentence.'"

Belle added, "Someone asked my Rick how long we had been married and he said, 'Being married is just like being in the army. You can't remember when you weren't.'"

Across the aisle, Marylouise reported: "I exercised for thirty minutes today—fifteen minutes looking for my sweat pants, ten minutes looking for my sneakers, and five minutes on the treadmill."

Glenna laughed and said, "I exercise thirty minutes a day. I take 180 ten-second walks."

"Well, that's nothing. When I exercise, I have to stretch and warm up before I stretch and warm up," Joyce said.

Mabel decided to entertain the group. "I got my doctor's permission to join a fitness class—an aerobics class for seniors. I bent, gyrated, twisted, jumped up and down, and perspired for an hour. But by the time I got my leotard on, the class was over."

They were still laughing, half way to their destination and climbing a hill, when a terrible blast shook the bus. Suzie ground the bus to a stop. Mabel thought someone had fired a gun at them.

Suzie climbed out of the bus and walked around it

until she located the cause of the noise: a blowout on the left rear wheel. Her shoulders were drooping and she was frowning when she climbed back on the bus to make the announcement. "I'll call the office and ask for someone to come fix this. If anyone has a cell phone, perhaps she will call the restaurant to tell them we will be late." She pulled out her phone and groaned. "I don't have service here! Who else has a phone?"

At least four ladies offered phones—but none of them had service either. "We must be in a blackout zone. I'll walk ahead to find a phone. Unfortunately, we are parked at a dangerous location and I dare not move the bus very far. No one over the hill will see us. I'm going to move us as far off the pavement as possible and I'll be back as soon as I can. Sorry."

She set up the yellow hazard triangles several yards behind and ahead of the bus, and started up the hill at a fast pace.

There were a few complaints but Eloise began to lead the group in singing.

While they were singing, Johnnie Mae surveyed the situation. She had worked in her ophthalmologist husband's office. She loved telling "the girls" about some of her duties and the time her husband sent her to the hospital to retrieve eyes from a donor to be used for transplants. Enthusiasm for singing soon played out. She stood up and walked to the front of the bus, then to the back.

She returned to the front, right next to Mabel. "Girls, we are a sitting duck for an accident. We have to do something about it. The bus cannot be seen around that curve," she pointed to the back, "and cars coming the other way cannot see us over that hill." She was a big woman and she folded her arms across her chest and looked intimidating.

For a minute no one responded. Carol, the Queen Mum of the club, said, "What do you suggest, Johnnie Mae?"

"We need to form a patrol, or whatever we want to call it, to alert drivers. I'll need at least three of you who can walk a short distance." Mabel thought Johnnie Mae was most impressive.

Beverle took off her hat. "I'll help."

"Keep your hat with you! Use it like a flag to warn travelers. Now, who else?"

Carol and Marylouise stood up. "Carol, you and Marylouise go to the top of the hill. Wave your hats and yell at the drivers that there is danger ahead! They will be sure to notice you! Beverle, you come with me."

As the four left the bus, Mabel and the others watched them. "Like an army patrol off to get help," someone behind her said.

They could see the couple on the hill but watching from the rear mirror, Mabel saw Johnnie Mae and Beverle disappear around the curve. "God go with them," she whispered.

Johnnie Mae was used to taking charge and Beverle demonstrated her technique later for a good laugh from the Glenners. "She took off her hat, and made a big sweeping motion with it while bowing from the waist. At first a few cars came by and we warned them to look out for the bus. A ton and a half stake-bed truck, loaded with landscape trees came into sight. Johnnie Mae and I waved our hats and the truck slowed down. The driver put on his brakes and we heard the brakes squealing and a hissing from the brake cylinder." Beverle continued the story, telling exactly what happened.

"'What's up?' a friendly, masculine voice asked.'

"Our bus is stranded just ahead and we wanted to warn you,' Johnnie Mae told him. 'We had a blow out.'

'I'll see if I can help,' he replied and began a slow movement around the curve. We followed. He pulled up right behind the stranded bus, and when he climbed down from his cab, he was carrying a tire iron."

"Well, I'll be," Mabel said. "That beats all."

"But look!" Eloise said and pointed toward the hill. "The cavalry is coming!"

Walking slowly down the hill were Carol and Marylouise, accompanied by a man. Behind them, a huge semi-truck followed very cautiously.

Suddenly there were three burly men wanting to help the fair ladies in distress.

"You all sure look purty," one of the men said. The first driver placed the jack under the rear end of the bus and the ladies on board felt the bus slowly lift. In no time they had the bus jacked up, the bad tire off and the spare one on.

All the time two of the men were working, the other man was entertaining the ladies. "You remind me so much of my Aunt Lucy," he told Mabel. "You look like her and you sound like her. And she is something else! Why, she must be 65 and still lives on the old farm by herself." He looked confused when the women began to laugh.

"She is a youngster. There is not a person on this bus who is under 80, and a couple are in their late 90's. Eloise, Lucille, raise your hands!" Carol said. "These ladies are both 99 years of age, and still going strong!"

"Well, I'll be dad blamed. You are all beautiful!"

Suzie appeared and stared at the parade. "You ladies having some kind of a convention?" she asked. "James is on his way, but Mrs. Devereux can send cars to take us home if anyone wants to go. Gosh! We surely appreciate you, men. I cannot believe you have the tire changed. I'll pull the bus up a little to an abandoned store's parking lot where we will be safe, and call for cars if anyone wants me to. James can take the flat tire back to have it fixed or replaced."

No one chose to go home. They preferred to wait for James, and continue their trip.

When the trucks had gone, Mabel suggested that they let James believe that Suzie had changed the tire, with the help of the Red Hat Ladies of Dogwood Glenn.

"Aw, he would never believe it." Suzie waved off the idea. "I called the restaurant and they will hold our reservations. How did you get those truckers to stop?"

"Aw, you would never believe it," Johnnie Mae said.

"But, I can tell you one thing that we can all believe," Beverle said, "Most people are incredibly kind to old people."

"Amen," whispered Mabel.

Chapter Eighteen

The next week a hot summer rolled in with humid, sweltering heat. Mabel refused to let it keep her from activities. On the Red Hat excursion, she realized how little time she had spent lately with one of her favorite people—Meriel Sorrels. She arranged a tea and Tucker volunteered to push Meriel's wheelchair to Mabel's apartment from Chrysanthemum Hall.

Mabel's flowers were nearly gone, due to the heat, but she did have a lovely hibiscus plant on her deck. The flowers were a vivid pink at the edges but faded to a light yellow in the center. She couldn't have a tea without a centerpiece, so she cut three branches and arranged them in a pottery vase.

She organized her tea service, and added a couple of mugs so that Tucker and Noah would enjoy her raspberry tea. She had invited Sam and Stella but they were going to be out of town. She invited Nettie and Grace. Her apartment was too small for more.

She looked over her guest list and was anticipating a cheerful afternoon. She would serve three kinds of her homemade cookies and the last of the chocolates that Tucker had given her. "Do I need to fix coffee?" she had asked Tucker but he assured her he and Noah could drink tea if she did not require them to drink out of a "toy" cup and raise their little fingers.

Meriel Sorrels, like Mabel, was a retired high school teacher. She had to retire from the job she loved because of a severe problem with peripheral neuropathy. One foot had been amputated, parts of nearly all her fingers in both hands had been removed, leaving her with badly deformed hands. If she complained, she did it in the privacy of her own apartment. Mabel always found her unfailingly cheerful. She was an extrovert involved with any activity that she could participate in. She had taught drama and Mabel heard she was helping to put the talent show together.

Mabel wondered if she were confined to a wheelchair if she could show such a optimistic attitude. Meriel was a glorious example of what people could bear if they had a strong faith and a supportive family. Everyone loved her.

Grace and Noah appeared together. She wore a turquoise blouse and a long crinkled skirt in a floral pattern. She looked like a beauty queen. Noah treated her like a queen, hurrying to pull out a chair for her. He took one near her.

Tucker had moved to the furthest corner, trying to stay in the background, but when the doorbell rang again, Mabel asked him to answer it. Nettie entered the room with a gregarious gladness that included the weather, the table, and all the other guests. She seemed unusually happy. The blue blouse she wore accented the blue of her eyes.

Mabel invited everyone to the table to choose their desserts and she had arranged a place where each could place their tea near an "easy chair." Meriel had asked to sit next to the table. "Would a different cup be better for you?" the hostess asked.

"How about a mug like the men have? Mabel, you always entertain so beautifully."

"I always have lovely guests that deserve the best," Mabel replied.

Meriel introduced a subject that they were all interested in. "Rachelle has asked me to co-ordinate the talent show and to direct the timing!"

"I'm one of the backup singers for Rachelle and we are going to have absolutely gorgeous gowns!" Nettie said.

Tucker asked, "Where are you going to get the 'absolutely gorgeous gowns'?"

Meriel and Nettie answered together. "Rachelle is donating them."

Nettie continued, "She let each of us take our pick from a dozen beautiful costumes she has worn in the past. She told us to have them altered to fit us. I'm still hunting someone to hem mine."

Mabel assured her, "I will be glad to hem it for you, dear."

"Who is on the program?" Tucker asked.

Meriel and Nettie again started together. This time Nettie yielded to her friend. Meriel said, "We are lucky to have two great pianists!" She pointed to them. "Noah and Grace are going to do a couple of duets."

"And, Noah is going to accompany Rachelle and the backup singers," Nettie said.

Tucker asked about Gevano. Did he have a part in the concert?

Grace, usually so quiet, responded enthusiastically. "He is a talented singer. He is going to start the program with an Elvis Presley interpretation and end it with a hymn."

Meriel told them that Rachelle had a magnificent voice, "But she says it's not like it used to be so she organized the backup group."

Mabel passed the tray of cookies around the room and Tucker refilled the cups with tea. He placed the sugar and cream on the coffee table.

Meriel teased, "You are certainly at home in Mabel's apartment, Tucker."

"I've been a henpecked husband most my life, so I learned to do what a beautiful woman asks me to do."

When the quiet laughter and teasing died down, Nettie unexpectedly turned to Noah. "You are a preacher. Right? Then answer a question for me."

"I'll be glad to try." Noah said. Mabel had warned him that Nettie might ask him some questions.

"Why are we so afraid of death?" Nettie blurted.

"I don't believe everyone is afraid of death. I'm not. I think, however, in the setting where we live, a continuing care community, we are more aware of death than some people. We hear of it frequently and ambulances are in our driveways more than we want them to be."

"Why are you not afraid to die?" There was a pleading in her voice and eyes.

"Because I believe in the Lord Jesus Christ and the knowledge that He will be with me when I die. He tells us He will be. Do you know Him?" he asked quietly.

"Of course. I have been in church and a believer most of my life. And I love your Bible study. It's just that …"

"Can I tell you a story?" Grace asked.

"Please do," Nettie answered, and looked around for approval from the rest of them.

"I'm not afraid of death because I died once, following surgery, and actually had an 'out-of-body experience,'" Grace said.

Everyone in the room stared at Grace, and Noah's mouth gaped open. Mabel was speechless. Grace continued in her soft, confident voice. "There was no tunnel nor a shining, bright light that I have heard described by other people. I was suddenly floating above my bed in the intensive care unit. I could see the surgeon, other doctors, the nurses and my husband and they all looked so sad. Then, I was aware of a Presence. I could not describe Him. He was wearing white but so were the doctors and even my husband wore a white jacket. I knew it was Jesus and He looked at me with such love and acceptance that He took away any fear I could have had."

No one spoke for a minute. Then, Noah said, "Wow!" He reached over to put his hand over Grace's briefly.

Tucker repeated it. "Wow!"

Nettie said, "Thank you so much for sharing. But you are a better person than I am. Perhaps He will not be there for me."

"Nettie," Mabel said, "I know He will be there for you. He has said He would." Then, she quoted John 3:16. "For God so loved the world that He gave His only begotten son that whosoever believeth in Him shall not perish but have eternal life."

Nettie bowed her head and began to cry. "You have all made me feel so much better."

Meriel had been quiet during the discussion. "If we make you feel better, why are you crying. I know. Because you are a woman." Now she laughed. "I can hardly wait! He has promised us a new body and that includes me!"

Tucker got up to offer more tea. "I think death is hardest on those of us who are left behind."

"Yes, you're right," Meriel agreed. "I lost my dear husband after only 10 years of a wonderful marriage—in a car accident. I have lost a lot of members of my family and some very dear friends. I wonder often why He doesn't take me."

Noah spoke, "All of us have been touched by death. In my case, my wife died in an accident that I was partly to blame for."

"What do you mean?" asked Grace incredulously.

"She was running away again. She and her lover took my new car and I called the police to report it. They were fleeing the police when the accident happened." Grace took Noah's hand in hers and she continued to hold it.

Nettie spoke up. "You all make me feel so ashamed. I don't think I can continue to be afraid."

"Would you like for us to pray for you?" Mabel asked. At Nettie's nod, she said, "Lead us in prayer, Noah."

And he did. He stood up and began with reverence. "Our wonderful God and Father, we love you and ask for you to bless each of us here. Thanks for Mabel and her generous gift as a hostess. We know you love us and that you bless our friendships. Please help Nettie to find the peace and lack of fear as she grows older. Help each of us to know You are in control and will take us home on your timetable and that You will be with us and love us into heaven. Please give each of us more faith. Amen."

"Amen," Tucker said. "I have the feeling we are all going to need it soon."

"Quit saying that, Tucker," Mabel chided.

He smiled, but his eyes were sad as he looked at her.

Chapter Nineteen

Song sparrows, in the maple tree outside her window, woke her up. Mabel lay in her bed and eavesdropped on the peaceful domestic conversation. There had been an enchanting time in her life when she and Will would waken to a similar sound. Will would slip out of bed and bring her a cup of coffee and the paper. He got his coffee and climbed back in bed beside her. Something caught in her throat. She reached over and patted the other side of the queen-sized bed. She felt a sudden yearning for companionship.

The years with Davis had been too busy for the luxury of an additional hour in bed. When she lost Davis, she never expected to marry again—and certainly after Will's death she knew she would be single for the rest of her life. She would be 80 in a couple of years and it would be unseemly to even think about romance!

Passion? How necessary was that? Passion was not to be confused with love. She remembered Pearl Buck had written years ago something to the effect: "We don't need less sexual contact, but more. Intimacy in marriage involves far more than the bedroom. It involves a shared joke, a quick touch, a smile that can supply a hidden message, buttoning a shirt." Pearl Buck insisted that any contact, however, brief can improve relationships. *Why do I feel lonely today?*

Mabel put her feet out from under the covers and sat up. She never dwelled on the past—especially since she had lived such a fabulous life. She felt that what time she had left should be used to help others. *Oh, that sounds Pollyannaish and I am as selfish as the next person.* Now she would have to hurry to get to the beauty shop on time.

There were few days in Mabel's life that didn't provide a surprise or an interesting tidbit of information. She had heard others complain that the beauty shop was a circulator of nasty gossip. Mabel enjoyed a lively conversation, but her friends knew she did not participate in hurtful gossip.

She was surprised to see Willie Dewitt on the porch with his sketching pad. She stopped to tell him Tucker had admired his "doodling" on the church bulletin. He was waiting for the bank to open and Mabel told him about the new art class Marylouise was organizing.

"Oh, I know. My work will have to be in black and white or charcoal because I don't have the supplies for watercolors or oils."

Mabel had heard that he was usually short on cash. *Well, I know someone who has more money than she knows what to do with. Let Etta pay for supplies. I'll have to suggest it to her.*

Mabel had seen enough of his work to know that he had talent.

She was surprised to see Olga Wegener in the shop. They didn't usually go at the same time. When Mabel spoke, Olga's answering smile said she had not held it against her that Mabel had confronted her about Barry.

Mabel was already at the sink when an aide, Pearl, from health care, came rushing in, pushing a wheelchair with Sophie in it.

"Her family is on their way for a visit and she really needs a hair washing! They throw a fit if she does not look her best. Could you work her in?" she asked Raymie.

Mabel moved out of the chair and motioned for Sophie to go first. Raymie thanked her. "I'll only wash and blow dry it, so it will not take long."

By the time Raymie was ready for Mabel, they could see that Sophie had eaten an abundant supply of candy, especially Tootsie Rolls. She had helped herself to the box Raymie and Bette kept for all the sweet tooths who came to the shop.

Bette reminded Raymie about how sick Sophie had gotten on another occasion from too many dips into the candy jar. There was a trail of candy papers all around her on the floor. When Bette started to move the jar, Sophie grabbed another handful.

Everyone had a good laugh about it and Raymie got the broom. Both Mabel and Olga were still in the shop when Pearl took Sophie back to her room—only to come racing back. "Did Sophie leave her teeth here?"

"Her *teeth*?" Raymie exclaimed.

Pearl replied, "She lost them." She made a quick search and was leaving when Bette shrieked. "Ugh! Here they are—caught between newspapers in the magazine rack. I won't touch the mess."

"How will I ever get the sticky chocolate out?" Pearl groaned.

Olga surprised everyone when she said, "I'll take

them and clean them."

"But they are filthy! How can you get them clean?" Bette asked.

"I'm a former dental hygienist and I still have some of my tools." She turned to Pearl. "Give me an hour, then come to my apartment at 201 in Bougainvillea Hall."

Mabel hoped she had hidden her astonishment that Olga had offered help. She followed Olga out of the shop. "What a fine thing for you to volunteer to do!"

"At least I have the tools and skill. Someone could wreck these dentures. It's a matter of professional pride."

Mabel told herself: *You just never know what people are made of.*

Chapter Twenty

Mabel checked the water level of her bouquet of white daisies before she answered the door at Tucker's tapping. Sometimes she would just call out to him to come in, but he was uncomfortable with that. *Tap, tap, tap—tap, tap.* He had probably drifted into Morse code—since he was a long-time radio ham.

Mabel didn't think it was necessary to follow all rules, if she felt they were silly, as long as no one was hurt. In spite of repeat warnings from the management to keep apartment doors locked, she didn't. She often left hers open a couple of inches. That saved her from getting up each time the doorbell rang.

She didn't know for sure, but she suspected that Tucker checked her door each night before he went to bed and reached in to turn the lock on. It was always locked when she got up each morning. She had never asked him about the practice.

Tucker came in rubbing his prominent stomach. "You are not good for me."

Mabel bristled. "I *told* you I found a recipe for banana pudding that is low in sugar and fat."

"Yeah. But, I don't believe it. It's always too good, not to be sinful."

"Sit down and try it. I had a little trouble with the meringue. I think my eggs are old."

"Then," Tucker said and grinned. "I won't touch it. Meringue must be perfect!"

It was like most of their beginning conversations, full of teasing and fun, but as the evening progressed, he seemed a little confusing to her and parts of what he said she would review for days to come. "Do you know what faith is?" he asked.

"I certainly know the Biblical meaning," she responded, puzzled.

"You may need to lean on your faith in the coming days."

They were both silent a few minutes and she wondered about what he was suggesting. She would think about it often in the next few days. "Tucker, why haven't you let me read your book about decoding messages?"

"That was not a happy time in my life. When I was working with the National Security Administration, I was essentially a spy. I'm convinced it contributed to Dorrie's breakdown years later."

Mabel realized it would be best if she dropped the subject but she persisted. "Ed has been so interested. Tell me about it." Later she wished she had been more aggressive.

"I can't. I'm sorry, Mabel. I can't partly because I don't want to remember that segment of my life and also because a lot of it is still secret. The work is dangerous and secretive. I know my Dorrie felt betrayed because I couldn't share with her. Yet, I knew my work was saving American lives. You must trust me, no matter what."

"You sound like you are still working."

He stood up and carrying his bowl of pudding, he came around to stand beside her chair. "Do you know that you are a nosy old woman."

"And you are an obstinate old man."

He laughed and changed the subject. "Any more duets from downstairs?"

She told him Grace and Noah were rehearsing for the talent show.

"When is Jeeves coming back for another run-in with Sadie?" He loved to tease her.

"That little altercation seems to have connected between Marylouise and Lloyd Ray. They are together all the time lately."

"It's good for both of them. Mabel, I would love to stay longer, but I have an important conference call in a few minutes."

"With whom?"

He shook his finger at her. "No, no, no. I told you, you are too nosy."

"Tucker," she whispered, "don't lead Ed into danger."

"My dear, you shock me! I love that boy. I hate to mention it, because you might claim the credit, but he is brilliant and a real gem. Go to bed, Mabel. Tomorrow is another day. Just another day," he added quietly, as though he expected her to remember it.

She walked to the door with him. "Now, don't you forget the symphony concert tomorrow. We are going to stop at Bellini's for lunch just before the concert."

He shook his head. "That restaurant is going to be my undoing." He leaned over and kissed her on the forehead. "Get some rest. You'll need it with the concert and lunch and all."

ꟾ

Tucker usually called before a trip to ask if he needed to wear a suit and a tie.

She was prepared to tell him to go with comfort; a

priority since it was an afternoon concert. He didn't call.

She knocked lightly on his door when she started downstairs. He didn't answer and she knocked much louder. No response. Just another day, she thought and cold chills crawled up her spine.

She took the elevator down alone, hoping he had gone early to check his mail. He was nowhere to be seen and his car was still parked next to hers. As she waited for the activities bus, perplexed and a bit miffed, Kim, of the sales staff, came by. Mabel explained the situation to her and Kim promised to check his apartment. If he was sick, she would call the activity director's cell phone and get a message to Mabel.

Why in heaven's name would he miss the symphony? Why hadn't he explained last night? He had been looking forward to hearing Vivaldi's *Four Seasons*, and had expressed pleasure that Grant Llewellyn was directing today. He shared that Dorrie had played the violin in the University Symphony.

The fine food at Bellini's was tasteless.

Mabel grew restless during the symphony, something entirely new for her, and wished she was home.

She skipped dinner. Much later, she called Ed's home. His wife Sue answered and told him Ed was on duty with the Army Reserve.

She gave up and went to bed. But, she couldn't sleep. Tucker Quick had simply disappeared.

Chapter Twenty-One

It was the third day since Tucker disappeared and Mabel was feeling a growing anger. She regretted ever introducing him to her son. In hindsight, she knew that Ed was involved and neither of them had trusted her enough to confide in her. Her resentment of Tucker festered. *If he has any plants that need watering, I'll just let them die!*

It wasn't like her to be childish, but she felt so *dumb.* Surely she should have seen this coming. After the second morning, she began picking up his newspapers and stacking them neatly in his outside hall closet beside the front door. He must be coming back, she thought, or he would have canceled the paper.

Few of her friends knew Ed was missing also, and when they asked about Tucker, she just shrugged, as though she couldn't care less. She felt like the decoding "thing" had something to do with it and she was determined to read Tucker's book, *The Code Breakers.*

She asked the housekeepers to let her into his apartment. She saw at once that his leather briefcase was missing. She reached to retrieve the book from the top of the desk, but stopped cold. Tucker had a picture of her, with Jeeves, framed and in a prominent position next to his book. She had no idea when the picture was taken or how he had obtained it.

One of the housekeeping ladies, Rose, teased her. "Are you Mr. Tucker's girlfriend?"

Mabel didn't even smile but took the book and hurried back to her apartment. She placed it next to her blue leather chair. She wanted to start reading it right then, but she was going to be late for the talent show. She dare not miss it after pestering everyone else to put it on.

She walked slowly toward the administration building which housed the offices, auditorium, kitchen and dining room. She didn't want to see or to talk to anyone and avoided friends who waved to her. She usually chose a place on the aisle, taking the second seat so Tucker would have more leg room in the aisle if he needed it. She pinched her lips together and sat in the middle of the last row. The auditorium filled quickly until there was standing room only.

Ushers were smiling and passing out the elaborate programs Marylouise had designed. Mabel sensed a festive excitement, but felt no part of the merriment.

Meriel was seated at the back with her stop watch. She had confiscated a large spot light and it was under the management of Lloyd Ray, who was noticeably awkward with it.

Matt rolled his wheelchair to the front of the auditorium. "Ladies and gentlemen," he began into the mike, "welcome to our first Dogwood Glenn Talent Show. Our theme is patriotic today since this week we celebrate the Fourth of July. Please stand and Phillip Sebastian will lead us in the Pledge of Allegiance to the flag."

Lloyd Ray turned the spotlight on, focusing on the large American flag. Phillip's deep voice led the pledge.

"We begin our program with a guest appearance of Elvis Presley!"

Lloyd Ray almost took a tumble and he tried to whirl around to put the light on Elvis, standing at the door.

Amid clapping, Noah played a rousing introduction as Gevano stepped into the room wearing tight white pants and a flowing white leather cape, lined in scarlet, with a high collar, singing "Jailhouse Rock." In the amazing costume, Gevano strutted down the aisle.

"The Warden threw a party. …

Let's rock, everybody, let's rock."

Stunned looks turned to surprise and then to pleasure. Mabel was a bit ashamed when all those old women began screaming and clapping. Etta stood up and Elvis threw her a green scarf. Mabel's impeccable etiquette made her wonder what had happened to decorum?

The spotlight followed Elvis, but the movement was jerky—which suited the seductive gyrations of his hips. He threw six more scarves and women were screaming for them. By the time he finished, nearly everyone was standing and singing the "Jailhouse Rock."

Mabel expected the next song would have to be another jarring Rock and Roll like "Hound Dog." She wished she could get up and leave unobtrusively.

She was pleasantly surprised when the clapping died down and Noah began a quiet introduction. Gevano began in a beautiful baritone:

"Love me tender

Love me sweet.

Never let me go."

He invited the residents to join him in the chorus. They finished with a melodic:

"And I love you so."

My! Mabel thought, *anything else would be anticlimactic. I'd hate to be on next.*

But Pete Grissom was not the least intimidated. Willie Dewitt, acting as a stage hand, pulled a chair out to center stage for him. Lloyd Ray focused his light on Willie and Willie threw his hand over his eyes as Pete sat down with his banjo on his knee. Amid chuckles and giggles, Lloyd Ray jerked the spotlight from Willie to Pete.

After playing his banjo, Pete pulled out his harmonica and played, "When Johnny Comes Marching Home Again."

Willie quickly removed the chair and the audience heard from The Dogwood Glenn Troubadours. They sang a couple of patriotic songs. They brought the audience to their feet.

Finally, Matt announced Rachelle and her choir. Marching in from the hall—eight senior ladies wearing gorgeous evening gowns made a dramatic entrance. Willie extended his hand and helped each up the stairs, with the spotlight wavering a bit. When they were in position on the stage, Rachelle stepped out from the stage door. Again, people were awed by an exquisite evening gown. As often was the case, Rachelle wore gold.

Noah began his introduction at the piano and the backup choir began to hum.

In a voice that gave Mabel goose pimples, Rachelle began:

"While the storm clouds gather far across the sea,
Let us swear our allegiance to a land that's free."

When she began the chorus, her choir sang with her.

"God bless America. Land that I love,

Stand beside her and guide her
Through the night with a light from above."

On the final chorus, Rachelle asked the audience to join her. Mabel had never heard the residents sing with such gusto.

When the clapping died down, Rachelle raised her hand to speak. "This next song was a request from Dr. Tucker Quick."

Again her choir began to hum as Rachelle began:

"I dreamed a dream in time gone by,
When hope was high
And life worth living..."

Mabel was not as familiar with *Les Miserables* as Tucker but she recognized the song and hoped that Rachelle would not realize he was absent.

There were other performers on the program but one that Mabel knew she would never forget was a duet by Noah and Grace: "Stars and Stripes Forever." The pianists were stunning and Mabel, while knowing they were both professionals, was impressed. She felt a special pride because she was instrumental in getting them together.

Before Matt announced the final number, he exclaimed about the talent at Dogwood Glenn. "We could get a booking on Broadway!" He thanked all the stage hands and gave special recognition to Meriel Sorrels and everybody who helped with the production. "And now," he concluded, "we will have the privilege of hearing Gevano Stanley as Gevano Stanley!"

He pointed to the doorway and Gevano hurried in, but he was wearing a white shirt and tie, and suit, in contrast to the Elvis costume. In his rich baritone, Gevano began:

"Oh, Lord, My God, when I in awesome wonder
Consider all the world thy hands have made."

On the third chorus, Gevano raised his hand to invite the audience to sing.

"Then sings my soul, my Savior God, to thee,
How great Thou art! How great Thou art!"

Mabel felt tears on her cheeks and slipped out before many people could see her. In the process, she saw several damp faces. She could see Ruthie Sue struggling through the crowd toward her. Mabel made a hasty retreat out the back door.

It had been an excellent concert. If only Tucker could have been here!

Chapter Twenty-Two

Mabel didn't want to go back to her apartment after the concert; it felt so empty lately. Instead, she walked the other way, along the front of the Administration Building. She tried to concentrate on the luscious pink and red of the Crepe Myrtles that were beginning to open, but she was not in the mood to think about flowering trees.

At the far end of the building, she sat down on a concrete bench in the shade and tried to recoup her thinking ability. She felt so confused lately. Almost as soon as she sat down she saw one of her favorite couples, the Bradleys, approaching. James was pushing the wheelchair for his wife of 72 years, Maudiline. It seemed to be making him breathless and Mabel begged them to rest a moment with her. James gladly sat down beside her.

Mabel knew their story. James was a mill worker in South Carolina when he asked Maudeline to slip away after work to marry him. He was 19 and she was 18. When they retired, they moved to Dogwood Glenn to be closer to family. Only a few weeks later Maudeline had a stroke. Partially paralyzed from the stroke and suffering with diabetes, they could not have made it without the unselfish attention their daughters gave them. They were there again when James developed a serious heart problem. Maudeline lived now in the health care unit and James had a small apartment on the third floor of the same building. They were the perfect picture of an enduring, happy marriage. Mabel adored them.

Maudeline's makeup and hair were always lovely and she wore bright, happy colors.

"Did you get to the concert?" Mabel asked them.

"No. And I wanted to," Maudeline said.

James explained, "Maudeline had to have some medicine and we just got through. Was it good?"

Mabel replied, "It was a lot of fun and some of the performers were amazingly talented."

"What about the opera singer?" Maudeline asked.

"Rachelle was wonderful. So was Gevano."

James asked Mabel where Tucker has been lately. "Is he sick?"

"He has been away on business." Mabel wanted to tell them the truth—that she had no idea where he was or what he was doing.

James continued, "He is such a fine man. Is it a courtship?"

She couldn't lie again—not to James Bradley. "I'm not sure, James. Tucker had a happy 61 year marriage. My two wonderful marriages were a total of 50 years. And why would a couple in their 80's even consider marriage?"

"I'll tell you one thing I have learned through the years. His wife is not coming back. Neither are your good husbands. I know they would want the best for you." James said.

"But—"

"I don't think love is age conscious. Even if I was 85 and just met Maudeline I would want to spend whatever years I had left with her."

Mabel could feel the heat in her face her heart began to pound. "I have never discussed this with anyone!"

Maudeline said, "James is like that. He can pull a confession out of anyone."

"I wasn't aware," Mabel exclaimed, "that it was a confession."

James seemed upset. "Oh, Mabel, I didn't mean to tread on private territory. I'm sorry if I embarrassed you. I sensed that something was bothering you and I wanted to help. It's none of my business. It's just that I want you to be happy. I know our days together are numbered, but I wouldn't want to waste a single day without being married to Maudeline."

Mabel smiled. "You didn't embarrass me; you helped me. I needed some counseling. I was afraid it was inappropriate for a woman of my age to be thinking of a possible third marriage. I don't want people laughing about that foolish old woman."

"Well, I'm an old man, 92, and I don't believe in coincidences. I believe God leads us and guides us. Did you wonder about why God placed you both here at this point in your lives? I know God will tell you what to do."

Mabel looked down at her hands. She had been twisting them. She relaxed. "Thank you. I know you will keep this confidential and I ask you both to pray for me. And for Tucker."

Walking back to Bougainvillea Hall, Mabel ran into two other couples who were facing difficult times. Giff was pushing his wife, Irene, in her wheelchair and singing to her. They had been married many years. A block further Marie was helping her husband George manage a walker. They were laughing. George had recently suffered a stroke. They had been married only a few years. None of the three couples she saw this afternoon considered the trials they were facing as huge burdens. They counted helping their mates a privilege.

Then, Mabel had another vision: She was being pushed in a wheelchair and behind her, walking and singing was Dr. Tucker Quick. Her heart was playing leap frog. Tucker. Where was he? Somehow, she felt he was coming back to her.

When she got home, the apartment didn't seem quite so lonely. Her heart was calm now and she smiled when she thought about James and Maudeline. What did God have in store for her? Would His plan include Tucker? He had spoken to her once about marriage and she had cut him off. Would he bring the subject up again?

Suddenly, her self-confidence deflated. Tucker had disappeared for eight days and hadn't bothered to tell her he was leaving. He couldn't care very much about her.

Chapter Twenty-Three

One evening, just as Mabel and her friends finished their dessert, she saw the head nurse, Darlene speak with the dining room manager. Brad nodded and pointed to their table. It had to mean an emergency and Mabel's heart seemed to retract into a hard ball.

Darlene was not looking for Mabel. She addressed Noah. "There is a woman who is gravely ill, and she wants to talk with you, please. She said you would remember her. Her name is Nettie."

"Oh, dear!" Mabel said. She recalled vividly Nettie's fear of death and how they had tried to help her.

Noah was already out of his chair. "Will you folks excuse me?" He hurriedly put down his napkin.

"Would you like for me to come with you, Noah?" Mabel asked and saw the relief in his face.

"Dear lady, will you? I have been away from the ministry such a long time!" He helped her with her chair.

Grace touched Noah's arm. "Be sure and let me know what happens."

"I will and each of you pray for me."

As they followed Darlene down the hall and through a private entrance to the Health Care Ward, Mabel remembered the worst thing about moving to a retirement center with nursing care was it had lots of older adults who get sick and die.

Darlene led them to Nettie's room. "Don't stay but a few minutes because she has already been medicated and she needs her sleep."

Mabel knew that Nettie had been sick and she had visited her in nursing care, but she had no idea that she was so ill. Her eyes were closed and she looked like a porcelain doll against the white pillow. Tubes connected to her arm kept a constant flow of medicine from the bags hanging from a stand near the head of the bed. A transparent nose tube brought the oxygen to her from a large metal drum. Oxygen had been added since Mabel's last visit.

Darlene said, "Nettie, honey, I found Rev. Malone and he is here with Mabel."

Nettie's eyelashes fluttered and Mabel took her hand. It felt cold and bony. Nettie opened her eyes and looked at Noah and then at Mabel.

Darlene whispered, "Don't stay long," and exited.

"You are not afraid, are you?" Mabel asked her.

"I'm not afraid. I just want the preacher to tell me what to expect." She held her other hand out to Noah and he moved to the side of the bed to take it between his palms.

"Nettie," he said, "heaven is going to be jaw-dropping glorious."

"Will it take long to get there?" she asked.

Noah smiled. "Are you like the little child on an automobile trip who kept asking, Are we there yet?" I'm not sure how long it will take; probably not very long. Maybe about as long as it takes to fall asleep."

Nettie seemed satisfied. Then, she asked, "Will the

little dog I had and loved so long be there?"

Noah asked her what the dog's name was. "The Bible tells us that we will be happy in heaven. If you need Bonnie to be happy, she will be there."

Nettie was not satisfied yet. "Rev. Noah, I haven't always been as good as I should have been. Will I be punished?"

Noah leaned closer. "None of us has been as good as we should have been. Punishment is an issue left in the hands of an incredibility loving God. He told us not to be afraid and He is to be trusted."

Nettie sighed. But she had one more question. "Will I know Mama and Papa?"

"I'm sure you will know them, but remember, we'll all have new bodies. We will be free from pain. We will have extraordinary bodies."

A nurse came in. "I need to take her vitals," she explained.

"Should I leave?" Noah asked.

"No!" Nettie answered and she clutched his hand tighter.

Mabel didn't need to watch the blood pressure monitor to know that Nettie was failing fast. She seemed to be very tired and was asleep before the nurse left the room.

Darlene returned and said, "Thank you for coming. She has had a lot of sedation and will sleep for hours. Go finish your dinner!"

"Will you please call us if there is a change?" Mabel asked.

"Of course, but remember that she is a very sick patient."

As they walked down the busy hallway, Mabel said, "Noah, you were wonderful!"

"I felt a strength because I knew you were there and

that you were praying," Noah replied, "Where is Nettie's family?"

"She never married and has only one sister, who is on vacation and nobody seems to know where," Mabel said sadly.

They continued their walk. Noah said, "I would like to talk to you about something. Where could we go and have a cup of coffee together?"

"Let's see if the dining room is closed. If it's open we can get a cup of coffee."

People were still eating and Brad gladly welcomed them. He gave them a seat in a corner where they could talk in private.

"Now," Mabel said. "What's bugging you, young man?"

"You cut to the chase, don't you, Mabel? I'm kinda nervous." He stirred his coffee. "I don't want to make a fool of myself. Do you think I'm too old to fall in love?"

Mabel must have blushed. She played with her coffee spoon. "Do you think I am?"

They both laughed, and their mirth was a tension breaker. "Grace is the most wonderful woman I have ever met—present company excepted. But she had a great marriage and I had a failed marriage. I wonder if she would even look at me."

"She looks at you, all right, Noah. I think the feelings are mutual, and my suggestion to you is to just give her a little time. Become her best friend first. And develop your friendship with Katlin. Remember also, the joy of love is in the loving."

"Yes, I remember reading, 'Loving is its own reward.'"

To Mabel's great relief, before he could ask about her

love life, Brad came to their table and told them he would have to close up.

They were almost to Bougainvillea Hall when Noah cleared his throat, "So," he commented, "I see that you and Tucker are close friends. Good."

"Don't be foolish. I don't even know where Tucker is."

"He knows where you are, I can guarantee it. He'll be back."

Chapter Twenty-Four

In spite of the fact that her doctors had warned Mabel to use her walker, she preferred her cane. Today as she walked to the pool with Ruthie Sue, she tried to enjoy the little flare that her skirt—cut on the bias—produced. She felt feminine wearing it and she hoped it would cheer her up.

Her mind was on Nettie. Nurse Darlene called her early to tell her that her friend had died during the night. "It was a peaceful, gentle death," Darlene said.

As they neared the Wellness Center, Mabel, preoccupied about Nettie, missed the step down at the curb. Instinctively, she used both hands to break her fall. She fell, face down onto the street, exclaiming, "Oh, no! Oh, no!"

A quick glance to her right wrist, and she knew from the bizarre angle that it was broken. Yet, she felt no pain. She felt numb. Extremely modest, she wanted to pull her skirt down, but she couldn't make her hands, or legs work.

Ruthie Sue was screaming and a crowd quickly gathered around her. Dr. Stella knelt beside her. "Don't try to get up," she said. "Boy! When you do something, you do it big!"

To Mabel's relief, Stella adjusted her skirt more modestly, but her leg was bleeding and her skirt was soaking up the blood. "How do you feel?" the doctor asked. To which Mabel, with outspoken irreverence, replied, "Like a stupid fool."

"Where do you hurt—besides your pride?"

"Just my head. My hands are numb."

Stella said, "We'll have to fix you a splint before you can go to the Emergency Room."

Mrs. Devereux broke through the crowd. "I have already called the EMS. I'm so sorry, Mabel. How did it happen?"

Ruthie Sue quit blubbering long enough to say, "Isn't it obvious? She fell down."

Mrs. Devereux ignored her.

Mabel explained, "I was acting like an idiot and not watching my step. I missed the curb."

Ruthie Sue was crying so loudly that Stella told her to move back behind the group. "Mabel will be fine, but don't upset her. She will hear you crying and think you are hurt."

ꕥ

Stella rode in the ambulance with her and Sam followed in their car. It was afternoon when Mabel was pushed in a wheelchair by Sam, with Stella beside her, back to her apartment.

"I'll order your lunch," Sam said.

"No, all I want to do is to lie down—if I can with this hideous cast. Why did they make it from my fingers past my elbow?"

Sam replied, "There are not many bones in your hand that were not broken. You are very lucky you didn't break both hands."

Stella said, "Ruthie Sue wants to come stay with you. Shall I call her?"

"Can you prescribe a gag? A big one. No, I don't want her. Charlene is on her way. She is planning to spend a night or two. Just help me to my bed, please."

"We'll check on you in a couple of hours, dear," Stella said.

"You have been wonderful! Thank you so much."

ঌ৩

For the first time in years, Mabel felt tears on her cheeks. She chided herself. It was foolish to feel sorry for herself; it was not her way to deal with problems. The wrist was properly set and causing no pain. She had received gracious care from Sam and Stella and the ER staff.

Charlene had taken off work and, as soon as she could make plans for her children and husband, would be on her way to take care of her for a couple of days. But, she couldn't get her mind off Tucker and Ed. What could Tucker possibly be doing with an army reserve unit? If that was where he was.

She tried to get comfortable, but it was impossible with the cast. She couldn't lie on her right side to sleep as she usually did, She felt so helpless! She lay on her back and she thought about Tucker. She had grown accustomed to having him around, and she realized, to her surprise, she missed him terribly. A deep black hole of depression enveloped her. *What if Tucker never came back?* He had told her to have faith, then deserted her. She muffled a sob.

"Oh, God," she prayed, "I have never allowed myself to wallow in misery. But, I feel so depressed."

She dozed and when she awoke, Charlene was sitting in the chair beside the bed.

ঌ৩

Charlene was having a hard time with her mother. Nothing pleased her. Never known for her patience, Mabel was nearly impossible to deal with. Charlene brushed her hair and combed it for her, and Mabel complained because she couldn't do it herself. Charlene went through her clothes to find garments Mabel could put on and wear with the cast. She finally went to the local department store and bought several large blouses that Mabel could use. Neither mother nor daughter could comprehend all the complexities to life the heavy cast on her right wrist and arm could cause. Her personal hygiene gave her the worst trouble. When Charlene offered to hire a nurse for a few days, her mother was adamant. She didn't want anyone hanging around trying to help her.

Eating was an ordeal. Mabel had always been fastidious, and it embarrassed her to eat with her left hand because she was so clumsy. Charlene went through Mabel's recipes and cooked several things she knew Mabel would enjoy including easy to eat sandwiches. She brought her up to date with all the activities her high school grandchildren were enjoying. Mabel had always shown interest in their school and sports.

Finally, Charlene tried a joke. "Rich said to tell you not to worry about stumbling. The only thing that cannot fall is a worm."

"Ask Rich how long it has been since he fell." The response was unlike Mabel. She sat in the big recliner and slept or just stared off into space. She insisted on holding Tucker's big book on her lap but she didn't appear to be reading. She explained to Charlene the arm didn't hurt, but the cast was extremely awkward. Her scraped knee was stiff and it did hurt. Charlene cleaned it each day and applied a fresh bandage.

To Mabel's relief, Charlene had worked on the skirt she wore when she fell, soaking it in cold water and finally getting the blood out. Charlene pressed the skirt and hung it back in the closet.

"You are a dear daughter, Charlene. I don't know what I would do without you."

The next time Charlene found her mother napping, she slipped downstairs to talk with Stella and Sam. "I've never seen my mother so depressed! I don't know what to do."

"There's not much you can do, dear," Stella told her and Sam nodded in agreement. "There are antidepressant medications, of course, but they aren't really indicated for situational depression like this."

Charlene continued, "But she hasn't been herself for days. She told me she felt so low she would have to reach up to touch bottom. I wonder if she was more badly hurt in her fall than we realize."

Stella patted Charlene's hand. "Has it occurred to you that your mother is more depressed about Tucker's absence than she is of her injuries?"

"And Ed is gone also." A light bulb came on in Charlene's mind. "Of course! She talks about Tucker a great deal but I thought it was more of a love-hate relationship. I know they are great friends—"

Sam said quietly, "I think you can scratch the 'hate' part."

"Oh, I don't know, Sam. After this episode, she might really hate him."

"What a mess! And I must go home today."

"Charlene, you go on home. We'll check on her each day. I think it would do her good to go to dinner with us tonight, or, if not tonight, soon," Stella said.

"Mom cannot use her walker because of the cast and

she is a little unsteady with just the cane," Charlene told them.

"We'll get her there," Sam said. "Between us like crutches—or in a wheelchair if she'll tolerate it."

"And I'll see that she has food she can eat easily," Stella added.

ꕥ

Charlene was pleased to find her mother with a visitor when she returned. Grace Guimares was sitting next to her and they were talking about Tucker.

"What is his book about?" Grace continued.

"It kinda matches its title. It's about men and women who broke codes, mostly during wars, and how they did it. But there is a lot I cannot understand."

"Perhaps some of it is written in code."

Mabel pulled the book onto her lap and held it there with the cast-covered right arm. She thumbed through a few pages and then she gasped. "I think you might be right! In each chapter there are paragraphs that seem to have no bearing on the rest of the content. I'll bet they are a code."

Charlene said, "I hate to interrupt, Mother, but I need to leave."

Mabel was silent a moment then she said, "I know, Darling."

"When do you think you can go to the dining room for dinner?" Grace asked.

Charlene said, "Yes, Sam and Stella want to take you."

"I'm not ready yet. I cannot push my walker with the cast and it is very difficult to eat with my left hand."

"Let me know when you are ready to go to the dining room," Grace said as she left.

Chapter Twenty-Five

From her home in Cary, Charlene kept a close check on her mom. Some evenings she dropped in and sometimes she brought her daughter, Katherine, or her husband. The visits meant everything to Mabel. They took her mind off Tucker.

One afternoon Charlene got off work early, so she drove out to Dogwood Glenn.

"Mother," she said as she entered the apartment. "I saw Marylouise and she begged me to bring you to see the art class and what they are doing."

"She has stayed on my back ever since she started. I have been using the excuse that I couldn't come alone. Would you like to go?" Mabel asked her daughter who was a fine watercolorist.

They walked slowly across the street to the Administration Building where the activity room was located. The only sound they could hear in the hallway was a whiney monolog by Corinne. "Oh, my goodness!" Mabel said. "I know Marylouise doesn't enjoy dealing with that talking all the time. Corinne doesn't have a brake on her speech apparatus."

Charlene looked mystified, and it was too late for Mabel to explain but she understood her mother's comment about Corinne before they left the room.

Mabel was surprised to see seven people in the room, including Sam Wyler. Willie and Etta were there; Lloyd Ray, Corinne, and someone Mabel was especially glad to see Olga Wegener.

Marylouise wore her white artist's smock over her green blouse. The blouse brought out the green in her eyes. She was bubbling with enthusiasm. "Come see what we are working on now. We did the vase today and next week we will add flowers."

The easel at the front held a large painting of a grass green pottery vase, and the paint was not quite dry. Next to the easel on a table stood the actual vase, glazed in "frog skin green." Mabel wondered if Marylouise was a better teacher than artist.

Olga and Etta wore large aprons: Corinne wore an oversized man's shirt over her clothes. Mabel determined quickly that some of the men needed aprons also.

"Go by and look at each artist's work!" Marylouise exclaimed, and then she introduced Charlene to those who had not met her.

Sam's picture of a green pottery vase took Mabel's breath away. He used brush strokes of different colors and it had a textured look. His shading gave the painting a three dimensional effect.

"I didn't know you were an artist!" she said.

"I never had time to play until I retired." He seemed totally relaxed.

Charlene admired his work. "You have a touch of Monet. I love it!"

As relaxed as Sam was, Lloyd Ray exhibited the exact opposite attitude. He tried to hide his picture.

Mabel didn't press him and moved quickly to Olga's

easel. Delicate and dainty, her picture showed talent. She represented the vase in a light blue green.

Etta's painting was as much on her apron as the paper. She had trouble with the shape and she explained that Marylouise helped her cut out a pattern. By folding a paper with one half of the shape drawn she was able to make a pattern with both sides alike. She seemed to have slopped the paint on with a mop.

When they stopped at Willie's table, Mabel first noticed a fine set of watercolors on his table and a wide collection of brushes. Etta winked at her and Mabel didn't comment on the supplies. Willie's vase looked like a photograph. He had obviously finished first because he was working on a sketch now.

"What great work!" Charlene exclaimed.

"The watercolor, or the pencil?" Willie asked, his voice full of excitement.

"Both! They are great. Come, see, Mother! The watercolor looks like a photograph."

Mabel eased over to look at his watercolor painting, then her eyes became glued to the sketch. It was of Etta and it was as fine a drawing as Mabel had ever seen. Drawn with confidence, each line added something to the overall effect. His shading was delicate and he had caught the essence of Etta, lips tilting up with a smile.

Etta began to laugh. "Willie makes me look beautiful!"

"You are beautiful, Etta. Especially when you smile like that."

Corinne painted a much larger vase in emerald green. She used bold, contrasting colors. She highlighted the sides with orange and pulled it into the vase until it presented a brown shading that rounded the sides and gave the vase shape. Clearly, she had previous experience with watercolor.

Charlene leaned over to study the painting. "Your bold colors remind me of Van Gogh's work."

"I studied Van Gogh's style while I was in Europe. He is a hero of mine."

"Do you know about his life?"

Yes, Mabel thought, *but we do not have time for a documentary now.*

Charlene thanked Marylouise and told her she wished she had time to become a member of the class.

Marylouise seemed ecstatic they had visited her class.

"Their art is as diverse as their personalities," Mabel told her daughter as they walked back to Bougainvillea Hall.

Chapter Twenty-Six

The meals at Dogwood Glenn were the highlight of the day for most residents, and Mabel had missed them. When Sam and Stella offered to take her in a wheelchair two weeks after the accident, she agreed.

A large majority of residents were on the "one meal a day" plan and chose the evening meal. In time, although residents were encouraged to move around, most people habitually went to the same table with the same friends. The meals were comparable to a fine restaurant and the wait staff were especially kind to the residents and served them in a joyful manner.

Grace quietly cut Mabel's steak and baked potato.

During the last few months, Mabel's table friends had consisted of Tucker, Stella and Sam, Grace and Noah. Tucker's chair had remained empty since he had been away. It served as a painful reminder to Mabel she had no idea where he might be. Mabel had leaned over to answer a question from Sam when the dining room became extremely quiet. The Executive Director, Mrs. Devereux, had come into the room and raised her hand for attention.

"Listen carefully," she said. "I don't want to scare you, but I need to tell you the West End Bank was held up just a short time ago and a man made off by foot into the woods. As you know, this bank is only a few blocks from here. The police have asked me to tell you to go to your apartments or cottages and lock the doors. Please go home and stay home. Do not be surprised if you see lots of policemen on the property. They will be here to protect you. If you need a container for the rest of your dinner, the staff will give you one. Any questions?"

"Is the robber armed?" Lucas asked.

"I'm not sure, but don't take any chances. If you see anything suspicious, please call security. Now move as quickly as it is safe for you to do so and I will guarantee you that security and police will keep you safe—if you do as we say."

The residents were strangely quiet as they exited the dining room. There was no hysteria but they walked in groups as they went to their homes. Mabel wondered if Etta and Ruthie Sue would be frightened but she had no intention of calling them. She didn't want either of them in her apartment tonight.

ഇ

After dinner, Mabel joined her "supper" group in Sam and Stella's apartment to watch a glorious gold and pink sunset. Mabel's only regret about her apartment was it had eastern facing windows only. She missed seeing the sunset on a regular basis.

In the friendly atmosphere of the Wyler's apartment, thoughts of robbers faded away. When Sam pushed her wheelchair back to 404, she felt perfectly safe, and told him he need not come in to check her apartment.

"Can I unlock your door for you?" Sam asked.

"No, it's okay," she said quickly.

The living room was growing dark—but she did not

remember leaving the bedroom light on. Perhaps Charlene had come to see her. She limped to the doorway and stopped abruptly. A man with a gray "Durham Bulls" baseball cap was going through her dresser drawers. He was tossing her lingerie all over the room.

She saw her intimate apparel on the bed and the floor. "What the devil do you think you are doing? Get out of my apartment!" Anger at the mess gave her a boldness she regretted quickly.

She had obviously startled the thief but he groped on the dresser and quickly found his small hand gun. He leveled it at her.

A cold chill traveled up her spine. Mabel felt a weakness that almost made her knees buckle. The intruder's eyes held a wild, glazed expression.

"*Dónde*—where is *dinero*?" He looked mean, and obstinate enough to take anything she had.

"That's for me to know." She glared at him and he glared back.

"I shoot you. *Dámelo.*"

Her mouth felt as dry as a soda cracker and a prickling in her scalp made the hair on the back of her neck stand up. "This building is swarming with policemen and the gun shot would bring them right here." *Why can't I just keep my mouth shut?* Her voice was unsteady and sounded strange.

He motioned her to back up. "*Va!*" Again, he demanded money. He hadn't shaved in days and he sounded desperate.

As she backed into the darkening living room, she tried to stall him. "I have forty dollars and I will give you twenty." She was trembling but trying hard not to let him see her terror.

"No. Total. *Donde*?" He grabbed her left arm. "*Digame* or I throw you to *la calle*." He yanked her toward the sliding doors of her deck. "*Pronto*!"

She dug in her heels, but she was no match for him; he was as strong as a bull.

Mabel felt completely helpless, she couldn't get in position to hit him with her cast. *I want to die with dignity. How can I if I am plastered all over the parking lot?* She did not frighten easily but she was shaking now as he dragged her toward the deck. She had told Nettie that she wasn't afraid of death. It wasn't death that scared her—but the thought of dying at the hands of this crazed criminal.

If only she had a weapon! *Please, dear God, tell me what to do,* she prayed.

The robber turned slightly, let go of Mabel and pushed open the sliding doors. Mabel was engulfed with the warm summer air. She slumped to the floor. She was no contest for him but, by hokey, she would make it as hard for him as possible. He might kick her to death—but if she could make him put down his gun, she might have a chance.

He swore in Spanish and dropped his gun as he tried to pull on her arm.

Suddenly, the overhead light snapped on and a deep, familiar voice barked. "Move away from the lady or I'll blow your head off."

The intruder gasped and glowered at Tucker.

"I'll assure you, I know how to use this piece. I returned from Afghanistan today. Kick your gun to me. Now!"

Mabel thought she might really faint.

There was a slight pause as the thief gave Tucker a piercing scrutiny. He wavered unsteadily. But when Tucker cocked his revolver, he sighed, and kicked the gun in Tucker's direction.

Tucker kept his revolver steady as he wrapped his arm around Mabel's waist and pulled her up. Her heart moved into full throttle and was beating furiously. She leaned back against his chest.

"Pick up the gun and give it to me, Mabel," Tucker said. "I'll keep him covered."

She didn't want to move away from him, but he gave her a slight nudge. It was as if someone else had taken over her body. When she leaned over to pick up the gun, she was thrown off balance and stumbled.

The man made a move toward her, but Tucker grunted, "Uh, uh." The robber jerked to attention.

Mabel felt aversion at the touch of the loathsome metal. It was steely and warm where the thief had touched it. She handed the gun to Tucker.

She pulled the sliding door closed and limped to her chair. Carefully, she began to dial with her left hand. She was so nervous that she had to redial. When she reached security, she leaned back in her chair and looked at Tucker. He was the bravest, dearest man in the world to her.

Within minutes, they heard running in the hall and armed policemen burst into the apartment. It took only seconds to handcuff the thief.

Mabel was relieved. Tucker placed his gun on the table. He came to stand beside her with his hand on her shoulder and she reached up to pat his arm. "You saved my life!"

"Ma'am, it was my pleasure." He bowed dramatically.

"Where's Ed?" she whispered.

"On his way to his beautiful wife. Should be there now. Your arm?"

"I broke my wrist. It's okay."

She had not one ounce of energy left and had trouble explaining to the police what had happened. While she was trying to describe the situation, Marylouise swept into the room.

"Mabel! What happened?"

Tucker answered. "She was being stubborn and refused to give the bum her money."

"Oh, Mabel! Did he hurt you? Tucker!" she exclaimed as she noticed him.

A policeman cleared his throat and Marylouise apologized for interrupting. She made a hasty retreat.

It seemed forever before the police and others were gone and Mabel could face Tucker alone. She couldn't remember any of the angry speeches she had imagined giving him. She stood up and he folded her into his arms.

"Don't leave me again," she said, fighting tears.

"I don't intend to leave again, and I want to tell you something wonderful. There will be no publicity, no recognition, but your son became a national hero this week."

She smiled, tears running down her cheeks.

"Don't cry, my Mabel."

She lifted her face to him and he gave her the sweetest kiss she had experienced in years. He had never kissed her on the lips before. She wanted to cling to him but the cast made it uncomfortable. Finally, she broke away.

"What happened here?" Tucker asked. "You didn't lock your door!"

She told him about Dev's announcement at dinner and then asked him, "Have you eaten?"

"Nope. I need to fix some coffee while you tell me what happened to your arm."

"I'd much rather hear about your adventure. But I guess most of it is secret."

He walked back to her and pulled her head to his chest. "Yes, nosy, it is. Sorry."

"How about a peanut butter and jelly sandwich?" she asked.

"I'd love one."

"Then, you will have to fix it yourself." Mabel held up her cast.

"Now, dear lady. Tell me how you did this!" He touched her cast, then pulled a chair into the kitchen and told her to sit down. "I'll bet that thing itches!"

"Fix the coffee while I tell you," she said.

He looked tired to her, but he was flushed with happiness. Wherever he had gone, whatever he had done, made him radiate contentment. To Mabel, he portrayed a victorious warrior.

"Tucker, you said Ed was a hero. How about you?"

He grinned. "I did all right. For an old codger."

"Oh, I wish you could tell me!"

"Just know that your country is much safer today than it was a week ago."

"The fatigue in your voice and face tell me you have had a long day," Mabel said.

Tucker was licking his fingers. "I can never make a decent peanut butter and jelly sandwich!"

Mabel laughed. "Next time don't spread the jelly all the way to the edge of the bread! How long has it been since you and Ed slept?"

"If you are trying to get rid of me, honey, I'll leave after I finish this sticky sandwich."

"Tucker, you know I'm not trying to get rid of you. I have been worried sick about you but I do want you to eat and go home before you fall over. I have had enough excitement for one day."

"Not only are you nosy; you are a bossy old woman."

"Yes, I am and I intend to stay that way."

Tucker washed his hands. "Good. I like you that way. Keeps life interesting."

He was almost to the door when she asked, "How did you know that man was in here?"

"I leaned into your hallway to tell you I was home and heard him say he was going to shoot you. I went to get my revolver. Look what has happened to you while I've been gone!" He pointed to her cast. He shook his head, sadly. "Pitiful. You need someone to take care of you." He gave her a quick kiss and hug, and locked her front door before he went to his own apartment.

Mabel leaned against the door and smiled. He was home. She felt a great excitement as she moved to the telephone to call Charlene.

Chapter Twenty-Seven

Mabel expected Tucker would sleep in until late. She paced the floor until noon and knocked on his door. It took him a minute to get to the door and from his disheveled look, he had just climbed out of bed. His hair, what little he had left, fell across his forehead. His pajamas were half unbuttoned and he was barefoot.

She stood in the doorway and stared at him. She took a deep breath and in a high-pitched, nervous voice asked, "Will you marry me?"

His wide eyes showed his surprise. "Right now?" He spread his arms and hands out in a mock appeal. "Not even a 'good morning'?"

She stood her ground in the doorway as he staggered back to a chair, appearing to be terribly shaken.

"Mabel, we have talked about this before. You were the one who said we'd kill each other."

"Yes, but, Tucker, Dorrie is not coming back, nor is my Will."

She was right, of course. She looked so fragile, almost pathetic, with those huge black eyes and that awkward cast. He scratched his head. "Tell you what I'll do. I'll take your offer under advisement."

Her jaw dropped and she made a little squeaking noise, like a frightened wren. Then, she turned on her heel and slammed his door so hard that every picture on his apartment walls was knocked askew.

"Mabel ... Mabel ... wait!"

He got to the door just in time to hear her door crash against the frame and he heard the click of her lock. He stood in the hallway, his face white with astonishment. He felt sick—like someone had hit him in the gut with a baseball bat. He stood gaping at her apartment door. *What had he done? What could he do now?* Apparently, Mabel was not in the mood for joking.

As he stood there scratching the top of his left foot with the toe of the other foot, he heard the "ping" of the elevator and sounds of conversation. He scurried back to his place.

He fixed some coffee, and settled in his recliner without breakfast. How had he messed things up so completely and so quickly? Of course he would marry Mabel—he intended to. He had already told her son he was going to ask her. It was just that he hadn't expected it quite this way. Not only had she beat him to it, he rather felt it was a man's place to propose. Not that he would have really turned her down if she had given him a chance to explain. Well, he would order her a dozen roses, let her cool down and call Ed for advice.

ഊଓ

Mabel thought about ignoring the ringing telephone as she entered her apartment. She did not want to talk with Dr. Tucker Quick. He had knocked the props from under her. But, the call could be from Charlene or Ed. With wariness, she picked up the phone.

"Mrs. Yancey? This is Janet Fuquay. I'm a feature writer for the News and Observer. I would like to do a story about your ordeal last night. Could I come talk with you this afternoon?"

Mabel hesitated. Last night seemed like an incoherent nightmare. Finally, she agreed. "The whole thing is muddled in my mind, but I'll be glad to tell you anything I can remember."

"Around two? I'll bring my camera. I'd also like to see the man who rescued you."

Mabel gave her his telephone number. *I'll let her talk to him.*

Heavens! Mabel thought as she put the phone down. *What can I do with my hair? What will I wear?* She was also distressed about Tucker being a part of the interview.

ꕤ

By two o'clock, Mabel had brushed at her hair with her one free hand and dressed in the pale blue pants suit she had bought the last time she had shopped with Charlene.

Mrs. Fuquay arrived on time and insisted that Mabel call her Janet. She had a friendly, bubbly personality. She wasn't much taller than Mabel, but not thin, and she wore dark pants and a gray sweater.

Moments later, they heard Tucker's *tap, tap, tap-tap, tap.* He didn't wait for Mabel to call to him but walked right in.

Tucker and Janet shook hands like old friends. Mabel wondered if the whole thing was a conspiracy to facilitate their reconciliation.

As soon as they were all seated; Tucker and Mabel on the couch and the reporter in Mabel's blue chair, Janet asked, "Was your arm injured last night?"

After a discussion about the broken wrist, the reporter got out her notebook. Mabel felt a little chagrined when the first question was: "How old are each of you."

Mabel answered quickly, "Just say we are over forty."

Tucker inserted, rudely, Mabel thought: "Double that and you'll be close."

He received a quick kick from Mabel.

Janet winked at Tucker. "That's fine," she said. "Mrs. Yancey, where was the robber when you first encountered him?"

"He was in the bedroom throwing all my intimate garments around the room. On the floor—on the bed. What a mess!"

The reporter asked, "Were you frightened?"

"First, I was mad. Then, I was frightened; I'm not used to having a 44 magnum thrust into my face."

Again, Tucker interrupted. "Er, ah, it was a hand gun."

The reporter winked at Tucker again.

"Well, whatever," Mabel said as she kicked Tucker's leg.

"How did you get involved, Dr. Quick?"

"I was just coming home from a long trip, saw the door was open and stuck my head in to tell Mabel I was home. I heard the guy threaten to shoot her."

Mabel continued, "When he said he was going to shoot me, I told him the police would hear him, so he said he was going to throw me off the balcony. He began dragging me that way."

"Did that scare you?" The reporter was writing furiously in her notebook.

"Being tossed off a fourth floor balcony would not be my favorite activity."

Janet continued, "What did you do? You must weigh

little more than 100 pounds and your arm is unusable. I would have been frightened to death."

"After he got the door open, I pretended to faint."

"That was clever," Janet said.

"Oh, Mabel is very clever," Tucker said and defended his leg by moving it before she could kick him again.

"That was when Tucker turned the light on and said," Mabel lowered her voice and mimicked Tucker in a gruff voice, "Let go of the lady or I'll blow your head off!"

"Did he?" Pen poised over her notebook.

"Blow his head off?"

The reporter gasped. When she quit laughing she commented, "Did the robber let go of you?"

"Finally."

Janet said, "I guess he learned not to break into a retirement center. I believe this is the same moron who tried to rob West End Bank."

"Yes, the director warned us at dinner. She said to go home and lock the doors."

Tucker added, "That bank is only about three blocks from here and most of the property between is woods."

"Did he get any valuables?"

Mabel complained, "No, but he surely made a mess!"

Janet paused, smiled and asked, "Did you sleep last night?"

"Yes. Tucker stayed with me for a while and I was quite tired. In fact, I slept better than I had in two weeks." She did not look at Tucker.

Tucker explained, "Her son has been overseas with his Army Reserve unit."

"Well, let's take some photographs. We could use the roses as a backdrop. Are they to celebrate a special occasion?" Janet asked.

Mabel said, under her breath, "Hardly to celebrate."

"I sent them," Tucker said quickly. "I've been away for a while and didn't know about her fall and broken wrist and hand."

"That was nice," Janet said as she took her camera out of its case.

"Oh, he can be a very nice man."

Tucker whispered, "Mabel, your sarcasm is getting old."

"Really?" She smiled for Janet. She was not smiling when she tried to get up off the low couch. She rarely sat there and the cast kept her off balance.

Tucker offered her his arm and, reluctantly, she took it. He kept his arm around her as they moved to stand in front of the roses.

Janet observed, "You seem to be very close. Have you been friends long?"

Tucker said, "Only since I moved in here eight months ago. I live right across the hall. I knew her husband many years ago."

Janet gave them a smile that indicated to Mabel that she knew they were more than close friends. "I see," she said.

Tucker asked, "When do you expect the paper to run the story?"

"Soon, I think. It depends on space and the editor. I hope you will like it."

Chapter Twenty-Eight

As soon as Janet left, Tucker said, “Mabel I have to go to my daughter’s home this afternoon and won’t be back for dinner. I want to take you to lunch tomorrow.”

“I have an eleven o’clock appointment with my orthopedic surgeon,” she replied cooly.

“I will take you to the doctor and then to lunch,” he insisted.

“Charlene is taking me.”

He was getting annoyed. “Call her and tell her I’m taking you. She doesn’t need to take off from work.” He didn’t wait for an answer, but hurried out of the door.

“Oh, goodness, I didn’t thank him for the roses,” she said out loud. She was disappointed that Tucker was not going to have dinner with their group tonight. *But lunch tomorrow?* She was a little nervous. However, she remembered, Tucker had once asked her to marry him—or he was about to when she stopped him by telling him that neither of them were ready for marriage, yet.

ꕥ

It was as lovely a day as she could remember, in spite of the heat. The mercury hovered around 90 degrees, but rain was predicted and Mabel was hoping it would cool things off. She dreaded the ride to the doctor with Tucker but she was determined to be tight-lipped since she felt so embarrassed.

Tucker made no reference to her abominable performance yesterday. They talked about the weather and there were long periods of silence in the car. Finally, he asked her about the talent show he had missed.

"Rachelle sang a song just for you. She said you had requested it."

Tucker said, "Did she sing 'I Dreamed A Dream'?"

Mabel nodded.

"Was she good?"

"Yes."

"How was Gevano?"

"Fine," she replied.

"Are you voiceless today?" Tucker asked. "I know you're mad at me. I'm sorry I couldn't tell you I was leaving. Actually, I didn't know when or even if I would be invited to participate."

Mabel responded, "It's okay. I had no right to an explanation. Turn here and Dr. Henry's office is in the first building on the right."

He stopped the car at the curb, climbed out, helped Mabel up the stairs and opened the heavy door for her. "I'll park and be right back. Do you want me to go into the doctor's examining room with you?"

"Course not," she said curtly and saw the pain in his eyes. She felt her face flush with shame. He didn't want to be her husband, but he was her best friend.

In the waiting room, they sat together in hard chairs and no place to rest her cast. Tucker found another chair with arms on it and he moved it over for her.

"Tucker," she asked a moment later, "is everyone staring at us?"

"Seem to be."

"Why?" She was mystified.

He rubbed his jaw. "We are just a good looking young couple."

Mabel noticed a man near them was showing his newspaper to the people seated near him. She was feeling sorry about her rudeness to Tucker earlier. "Did I tell you that Nettie died?"

"No! When?"

"It was the day before I broke my wrist. Darlene came to the dining room and asked Noah to go see her and I went with him. Tucker, he was wonderful! He took her hand and reassured her. She wanted to know if her little dog would be in heaven." She was unaware her voice had warmed up considerably.

"What did he tell her about the dog?"

The nurse called her before she could answer, but she paused at the door. "He said she would be if Nettie needed her to be happy." Then she added, "Tucker, come with me. Two sets of ears are better than one."

He bounded out of his chair, surprising Mabel so much she laughed.

ᘓᘐ

X-rays showed that Mabel's wrist was healing nicely. The doctor thought they could put on a smaller cast in a week or two. Mabel seemed much more relaxed when Tucker drove her to the Majesty. Mabel knew it was a high-end restaurant, and in spite of herself, she got a little excited.

The waitress led them to a corner table, near the window. A potted orchid graced their table. From a long stem, it displayed seven lovely lavender blossoms. Next to her place she saw an orchid corsage with a large purple cattleya bloom. The table featured gold chargers and each pale green napkin was encircled with a gold napkin holder. The crystal glasses were rimmed in gold. The tablecloth was pale green also.

Mabel sighed. "Oh, Tucker, this place is elegant." She put her right arm on the table to get support for her cast. "But, how can I eat here without embarrassing both of us?"

"You couldn't embarrass me if your tried. It is all taken care of. I called Charlene and she made a suggestion. Just relax and enjoy yourself, my dear." He summoned the waitress, who offered to pin the corsage on for Mabel. "I preordered, Barbara."

"Oh, yes. I know. You didn't say what the lady wants to drink."

As soon as they gave their order, Tucker took her left hand. "I'm old and I cannot do lots of things I used to do. For instance, if I knelt, I couldn't get up. So, I'll just sit beside you and look into those black, mysterious eyes and ask you to marry me. Mabel, I realized while I was gone how much I love you and how foolish it is for us not to have the joy of a happy marriage in these last few years of our lives."

She caught her breath and gave a little gasp.

"Mabel, dear, will you marry me and share the remaining years of our lives with me?"

Before she could answer, he continued, "I've already asked Ed to be my best man."

"Well, then why even ask me?" She hoped she appeared haughty.

"Will you?" He sounded anxious.

She lifted her chin, but did not look at him. "I'll take

your offer under consideration." She calmly stirred her coffee and ignored him.

He looked deflated.

"Oh, I'm sorry," she gazed at him. "Do you mean today? I'd like to get this cast off before we get married."

He laughed. "I deserve that!"

She smiled. "We may be foolish old people but yes, for better or worse, I'll marry you."

Tucker turned to the people in tables near them. "Mabel has just agreed to become my bride!" In front of a restaurant full of cheering people, he kissed her. Including the customers in the celebration pleased them.

"Hey, aren't you the couple in today's paper? You saved her life!" a red-headed man said as he pointed his fork toward Mabel.

Other people clamored around, asking details about the would-be robbery and rescue. When things calmed down a bit, Mabel asked, "Have you seen the newspaper?"

"I glanced at the headlines but didn't open it."

Mabel said, "I left mine folded on the table to read when we get home."

Tucker chuckled, "Looks like we are in for a treat."

"I brought you a lovely sampler." The waitress set the sampler down and smiled at Tucker. "It is a plate of several of our best sandwiches, cut into bite size. He said you could eat much easier if you could pick up the food."

"Thank you, Barbara."

"Tucker! I am amazed and suddenly very hungry." Daintily, she sampled a tiny sandwich. "I am surely glad I agreed to marry you! You must come here often to know the waitress's name."

"Honey, her name in on the name tag she wears."

ꕥ

"So what did you think of Ed's work?" she asked later.

"I can only tell you when Ed gets 'on task,' he can keep his focus with all hell breaking loose around him. He is as sharp as a whip."

"Tucker, you must know that a way to a woman's heart is to brag on her children. Ed idolizes you."

Tucker was silent a moment and then he said seriously, "I know he is Davis' son and I'd never intrude on that, but Mabel, dear, I love that boy."

"So do I. Charlene is crazy about you also."

He bowed his head and grinned. "And I'm crazy about her. You'll love my boys when you get to meet them. And you have already told me that you think Jeanne is lovely."

"Indeed she is. I already love her," Mabel said. She knew that Tucker's oldest son was president of a mission college in Japan and his younger son was with the army in Germany.

Seconds later he added, "I never thought I would get married again. I never planned to. I had the mistaken belief that first love was a kind of vaccination that immunizes a man from ever catching the disease again. Then I met you and you drove me crazy."

"Are you saying you have to be crazy to marry me? Well, I guess you do, but I cannot help that. I won't be Dorrie. I cannot take her place in your heart."

"No, Mabel," he replied, "you will fill Mabel's place. What changed your mind about marrying me?"

"I was deeply depressed because you were gone, and that made me so lonely. I felt lost without you, Tucker. I spent a lot of time in prayer and I had a long talk with James and Maudiline Bradley. James told me love was not limited to the young—nor restricted by age. They have been married for 72 years. He made me realize Will would approve also. By the way, I passed the counsel on to Noah. He is in love with Grace."

Tucker nodded and expressed his pleasure, then thoughtfully he said, "I, also, prayed a lot. And I thought about Dorrie, and I asked myself what Dorrie would want me to do. I realized Dorrie would want me happy. She was sick for many years and didn't even know me in the end. But, I feel her blessings and, Mabel, as bossy and saucy as you are, I love you."

They didn't talk about setting a date or where they would live. They each wanted to savor the knowledge their future would be less lonely.

ꙮ

On the way home she asked him why he had rejected her the day before.

"I was flabbergasted and half asleep. If you had stayed a minute longer and let me catch my breath, I would have said, 'Yes, my dear, I want to marry you.' I had already planned this lunch date."

"Please, Tucker, don't ever tell anyone about my barging into your apartment yesterday, unintelligible and acting like an idiot!"

He put his hand over hers and slowed down. "I'll prize those moments forever. If it embarrasses you, I won't share it; but, Sweetheart, I was the one who goofed up." Silent for several blocks, Tucker then continued the conversation. "While I was gone I thought of something Longfellow wrote: 'It is difficult to know at what moment love begins; it is less difficult to know it has begun.'"

"When did it begin for you, Tucker?"

"You won't believe it. I first began to feel tenderness for you on the day we found the 'body' from the pool. I figured that if you worked that hard to help Ruthie Sue, you must be a gentle and caring person. I appreciated your spirit, and I kinda liked the guts you showed that day!"

"Even when I bossed you to pieces?"

He grinned but said nothing more.

Minutes later, Mabel exclaimed, "Look at the clouds! We are going to get our rain!"

"And here it comes," he said as the first drops hit the windshield. "What a priceless day for me, my wonderful Mabel."

"Wait! I forgot my doggie bag."

Tucker put on the brakes. Almost as fast, he sped up. "You didn't have a doggie bag. You don't insult the Majesty by leaving one morsel of food on the plates."

"I know," she confessed. "I just wanted to tease you. Thank you for the lunch and the corsage is gorgeous."

Chapter Twenty-Nine

Tucker followed Mabel into her apartment where she quickly grabbed the newspaper and with his help, spread it across the table. Below the fold on page one they read:

Don't mess with these seniors!

Rudolfo K. Rios learned not to try to burglarize the apartment of 78-year-old Mabel Yancey, at Dogwood Glenn. Neighbor 85-year-old Dr. Tucker Quick came to her rescue. Police say …

"Oh, my goodness!" exclaimed Mabel in mock surprise. "I look like an old woman."

"And I look like a bull that has just escaped the slaughter house."

They began to laugh. "Old age is an incurable disease," Tucker said.

"But what is more honorable than old age?" Mabel said and sighed, "At least for other people. Oh, I forgot. I must call my children."

He kissed her the same way he did on his return from Afghanistan, with passion. "I could get accustomed to that," she thought as she shooed him out. "I have to rest before dinner."

Her answering machine was blinking. Probably everyone in town had seen the photo and story except Tucker and herself. The first call was from Charlene, and she was excited about the story. There was a call from Ed and at least two thirds of the residents at Dogwood Glenn. Her pastor had called, as had her dentist. The machine was full. Thank goodness there wasn't any more room for: "Oh, Mabel, I couldn't believe it!"

She couldn't get the corsage off. She tried taking her dress off with it still pinned to it but she couldn't. Ruthie Sue had been there earlier and helped her get the dress on. She would never get used to the cast. Finally, she smoothed the dress as best she could and folded back the blankets and lay, very gently, across the bed. She intended to read the rest of Janet's news story but fell fast asleep. She dreamed Tucker had turned her down again. She woke up in a twisted sheet and happy it had been a dream only. It was nearly time for dinner.

She fretted about her dress being wrinkled, but there was nothing she could do about it now. She would ask Stella to help her take it off after dinner. She pulled out a simple strand of pearls before she realized she could not manage the clasp. She handed the necklace to Tucker when he came and asked him to fasten it.

Tucker commented about how hard it must be to take care of herself with the cast. "I wish we were married already and I could help."

"Does my hair look all right in back?" she asked.

He made a claw with his hand and tried to comb the back of her hair.

Laughing, she asked him if he had read the entire story about the robbery.

"That reporter made me sound like a hero!" he complained.

"You are! You saved my life."

"The revolver was the hero. Is that rescue why you promised to marry me?"

She pressed her lips together and closed her eyes. "Let me think. Yes, that among other things."

They walked to the dining room with Stella and Sam. At the door, Tucker held back for the Wylers to enter. He took Mabel's hand and they moved into the room—to the applause of 100 diners. "Welcome home, Tucker!"

He bowed and thanked them. "I am so glad to be home!"

Mabel smiled at him and felt fluttering in her heart. Thank goodness no one knew about their plans yet. She felt like she was a very young lady once again.

Chapter Thirty

Tucker barreled down the hall, walking faster than his usual gait, calling her name before he got to her door. "Mabel, honey, wait until you see—" He stopped suddenly. Her door was open and he could see that someone had cleared out all the furniture in the front bedroom. "Mabel, sweetheart—"

She appeared in the doorway, holding a dust cloth, her hair protected with a white satin night cap. "Charlene called right after you left and asked to come this morning rather than the afternoon. They wanted the bedroom set up before Katherine got home from school."

"But, I wanted to be here to help them. I wanted to see them. Did the whole family come?"

"No, just Charlene and Rich, and two friends to help. They were willing to move your desk and radio things."

Tucker looked back at his door. "Should have left you the keys to my place."

"My 'soon-to-be husband,' we would not have touched your things without your being here." She smiled at him and wrapped her arms around his waist.

"Watch it. I might take advantage of you if you treat me like this." He bent his head to kiss her and folded her in his arms. Then, he swung her around and gave her his news.

"What were you so excited about?" Mabel asked him.

"Oh! Let me show you some drawings. Willie Dewitt wanted to do something for us as a wedding gift. But, before I show you, we are under no obligations. If his drawings do not please you, the whole thing is off."

She looked up at him with her eyes wide. "The wedding is off?"

He began to laugh and so did she. He reached over to pull her hair net off. "I got into trouble about your purple night cap, I don't want to do it again." He handed it to her and walked to the table and spread drawings out. At first they made no sense to Mabel. "What are they?"

"Designs for our wedding rings. Do you see how he has entwined our names together. Your name is nestled within mine."

Mabel pushed her glasses back up on her nose. "How elegant. But could anyone engrave rings to include his beautiful designs?"

"That's why I'm so late. We went to the jeweler and Samantha asked him if he had any experience with jewelry design. She was thrilled with his drawings and told him she would like to hire him for more designs!"

"They are exquisite! I love them. They are unlike any other wedding bands I've ever seen."

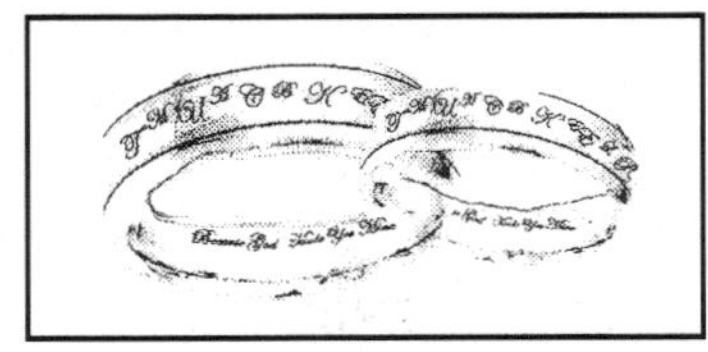

Tucker put his arm around her. "Willie confided in me that if he didn't get some kind of work, he might have to leave Dogwood Glenn. I told him he ought to sell some of his other drawings and we went by the gallery and they are interested in seeing his work."

"Tucker?"

"Yes?"

She was rubbing her fingers that extended beyond her cast. "Before you order the rings, are you sure we should do this?"

"Honey, I don't believe in living together without the benefit of marriage, and I intend to live here with you. Do you have doubts?" He studied her face, his brow wrinkled with worry.

"No. I am sure! I have never doubted I love you dearly." She smiled and lifted her face to him.

"Then, let's not discuss it anymore." He leaned down to kiss her.

"My loving husband-to-be, come look to see if this room is large enough for your office."

ꙮ

"Tea or coffee?" Mabel asked him and they sat down at the table.

"I always prefer coffee. How can you switch back and forth so easily?" He carefully folded up Willie's drawings.

"Tucker, I wish we could have just a small wedding—in Ed and Sue's garden with just family present. People keep asking me where it will be. It's not like I was wearing white and a long train and had a dozen bride's maids."

"We could just elope. That always sounded romantic to me."

"Are you serious?" she asked, scrunching up her face.

He smiled and leaned over to kiss her cheek. "No. I take our marriage very seriously."

Mabel told him, "I asked Charlene if she was embarrassed because I was getting married for the third time."

"And?" he questioned, "What did she say?"

Mabel giggled. "She reminded me I said once you were crazy." She grew serious. "She said since I was marrying you, she is delighted."

He patted her hand and sampled the coffee. He would have to take over this task. Hers was always too weak. "Our engagement is different in that most of the community saw us sparring, then, growing together, and falling in love. They feel like they are a part of it! Even housekeeping is abuzz. Barry, from maintenance, asked if he could come."

"But, it's our wedding and we can do what we want to," she protested.

"Yes, dear, but we could give to the community that brought us together."

Mabel made a face. "I don't need all that falderal. I just want you and our children with Noah to perform the ceremony, Rochelle to sing, and Grace and the Wylers—"

"And … and … and … Go on, Mabel. No private home garden could hold our crowd."

She rubbed her fingers together. "No, I suppose not. What do you suggest?"

He took another sip of his coffee. "How about leaving it all to me?"

"The groom in charge of the wedding? I am aghast!" She slapped her cheeks.

"What is so hard about planning a wedding?" he asked.

"Oh, Tucker would you do it? I have fretted and worried—"

"Sure, I'll do it. I'll appoint a committee which will include: my Jeanne, your Charlene, Stella and Grace."

"I'm going to leave it to you!" She didn't have the slightest doubt that he could pull it off perfectly.

Chapter Thirty-One

Tucker let his apartment door slam. He leaned back against the panel and took a deep breath. *Oh, God! What have I done?* He was not using God's name in vain. He felt desperate and was pleading for divine help. *What on earth do I know about planning a wedding? What possessed me to offer? Just calm down, old man.*

"God tell me how to handle this."

He thought of Mabel. How he adored that woman! He wanted to protect her, provide for her and to love her. She seemed stressed since her fall, but the cast would come off tomorrow. He held his large hands together gently as though a small bird nestled in them. I love you, Mabel!

He slumped down in his recliner. Thank goodness his chair would go to the other apartment. Mabel had been generous, giving him all the space he needed. He reached for his ever ready notepad and began a list:

Minister—Rev. Noah Malone

Location?

Flowers?

Chairs?

Ushers?

Wedding napkins?

Tucker stopped there. "Napkins" indicated food and he had no idea what to do about that. Jeanne would know so he dialed her number. And Charlene would know what to do also. But the wedding had to be special. He wanted the very best for his Mabel.

ꙮ

Mabel stepped out on her deck and sat down in her "garden chair." *You would think that someone who had already been married twice would know all the answers,* she told herself. She failed, as usual, to acknowledge that she was much younger when she married before. She had worked herself into a stew searching around in her apartment to make room for Tucker's things.

Tucker's things. Tucker's clothes hanging in her closets. *Tucker. He is a gentle man of faith, so kind and so patient with me. God has blessed me again.* She prayed that she would be worthy of him.

Back in her kitchen she looked at the clock and gasped. She had to hurry or she would be late for physical therapy. She had just assumed when they took the cast off she would be like she was before the fall and break. But the doctor ordered four weeks of physical therapy. In P.T. she caught balls, threw balls, squeezed balls and did hand exercises over and over again. Some fingers were still a little stiff, but she had noticed tremendous improvement. *Goodness gracious, I would be a complete wreck if Tucker had not offered to take over the wedding preparation. This is not like me. Why am I in such a tizzy?*

Mabel had looked through close to a hundred catalogs and been unable to find a wedding dress to suit her and the wedding was only two weeks away. However, after her session with the physical therapist today, Stella and Grace were taking her shopping.

ꙮ

Charlene came the evening before the wedding to spend a little time with her mother. They went to the bedroom to see the lovely aquamarine silk chiffon dress and shoes to match. The dress had a full skirt and long sleeves.

"Stella knew exactly where to shop," Mabel explained.

"She certainly did!" Charlene said. "The whole outfit is gorgeous."

Mabel asked her daughter if she know where the ceremony would take place.

"I do, but I can't tell you. It will be a wonderful surprise. Tucker has worked himself to death and worked everyone he knows to get things right."

Mother and daughter climbed up on the bed. "Do you remember what you and Dad told me before my wedding?" Charlene asked.

"Of course. We told you if Rich abused you to come home, but if he was a good husband, no matter how you might want to leave some time, you had to stay and make your marriage work."

"Yes, but I knew I could come home anytime. Dad would never turn his back on me, no matter what he said," Charlene remembered.

"You were the apple of his eye. You could wind him around your little finger, just as you can Rich."

Charlene adjusted the pillow so her mother could lean back on it. As Charlene had grown up, they had used her mother's bed for long, intimate talks. "I'll give you some advice. If you get mad at Tucker, and you will, just ask yourself if life would be better without him. I remember you called him a nut, crazy and looney when he first came."

"I didn't know him well, and you have to admit he can be crazy at times."

"I know how much he loves you and you love him," Charlene said. "All of us love him."

They shared a few humorous things he had done and said. "Mother, I came to tell you how much I love you and what a wonderful mother you have been." She leaned over to kiss her. She curled up next to her mother.

Mabel touched her red hair and continued to stroke it as they talked. "You are so like your father sometimes."

"Do you ever think of Dad and miss him?"

"Of course I do, especially when I'm with you and Ed. He was a wonderful man and I loved him dearly. Tucker talks about him sometimes."

Charlene took her mother's hand and encased it between hers. "How many meals have you cooked with these? How often have you hemmed a dress or skirt for me?"

Mabel knew she was looking at the brown age spots and noting the thin skin of old age that bruised so easily. "There is only one thing I'm worried about. Charlene, I do not want to bury another husband!" Mabel's voice broke.

Charlene was quiet a moment. The possibility had worried her. "As you have always told me, Mother, your way is to trust our God."

They were quiet a few minutes and the tranquil dusk was edging its way into the room. It gave each of them an intimate, quiet feeling. Neither wanted to reach for the light switch.

"Tucker says we have only a few years to share together but we will make the most of them," Mabel said.

"We might even spend all our children's inheritances," she teased.

"I'm not concerned about that. … Ed and I, and I know his children also, want you to have a glorious life. Spend everything. Go on a cruise. Book a flight to the moon."

"Now you are stretching it, my dear!"

They didn't hear Tucker's, *tap tap, tap-tap,* so he yelled out, "Anybody home?"

"I'll go home so you can have a little time with Lover Boy."

"He will have a fit if you do not stay and have some coffee and cake before you leave," Mabel said.

Tucker yelled, "I heard that and yes, I will. You must stay a little while to fill me in on how I can keep from annoying your mother."

"Just don't get her a cat!"

Chapter Thirty-Two

Pink clouds were turning to gold when Mabel woke up. She pulled her robe around her shoulders and went to the window. "A golden morning," she said out loud. She had developed the habit of speaking out loud when she was alone. She felt joy circulating through her veins. On such a momentous occasion, shouldn't she feel nervous? She was filled with peace. She had not the slightest doubt that she and Tucker had made the right decision. How amazing it was that love had come to them again late in life. "God is good," he had reminded her last night.

When married to him, she would be able to share more fully in the greatness of his heart and appreciate his quick mind. Dr. Quick and his quick mind. Funny, she had never thought of it that way.

They had chosen Saturday morning at eleven because they knew family and staff would be off work. She still didn't know where the ceremony would take place. She hoped it would not be far.

When Ed and Charlene and their families arrived just after ten, she felt relieved. She loved having them around and the fact that they so completely approved of the marriage made her feel especially blessed. "Where are you going on your honeymoon, Grandmother?" Katherine asked.

"Not anywhere special. We just want a few days at the beach and then Tucker wants to go by his old university. We don't want to be gone long. Charlene, you chose the perfect dress. Your pale yellow pairs beautifully with my light blue-green."

Danny came running in from the deck. "Come quick, Grandmother, and see what they are doing to your car!"

Mabel, her grandchildren and Charlene leaned over the railing of the deck. "They are painting 'just married' on the car and look at that long rope of tin cans they are tying to the bumper! Want me to go scare them off?"

"No, Danny, everything is okay. Let them have some fun. Tucker certainly is."

Ed asked if her suitcase was ready and he slipped it out of the apartment. By 10:30am Mabel was getting restless. "Hadn't we better be going? I have a wedding to go to!"

"No," Ed's wife, Sue assured her. "We don't have to go far."

Her family sat around drinking coffee and cokes as though it were a regular day.

Finally at 10:45 Charlene said, "The rest of you had better leave. Mother and Rich and I will be down soon."

"Is your corsage secure?" Charlene asked. "The yellow orchid is perfect, and I love my purple one. Tucker must have a thing about orchids."

"Let's be off," Rich suggested.

They went down the elevator, but instead of turning toward the front door, Rich led them to Etta's apartment door. "What on earth?" Mabel asked.

Then, she saw. From Etta's French doors, she could see dozens of people seated on folding chairs on the green lawn located between Bougainvillea Hall and the red brick security wall at the rear of the property line. The chairs faced a pergola, its latticework woven with vines and yellow mums. Across the front, were potted chrysanthemums—yellow, bronze, orange and maroon. Tucker had created a garden in his own back yard!

Mabel took a deep breath. As she scanned the group, she recognized that Cory, Ryon, Brendon and Mike, of the wait staff, were seating people. They were used to handling the walkers, scooters and canes, and they seemed to recognize that walking in grass was a feat for people who had trouble standing or walking.

Mabel saw friends from Dogwood Glenn, as well as people from her church. She recognized staff members and picked out Felicia and Evelyn, her housekeepers. She could see members of the kitchen staff and she was almost overwhelmed by the crowd. Barry was there, seated next to Stella and Sam. An overflow of guests were standing close to the building and next to the brick wall. She felt a lump in her throat. It was her family out there—her family of friends. She had wanted a family wedding in a garden and that was exactly what Tucker was giving her.

"Okay, Mother, let's go," Charlene whispered.

Rich opened the door and they stepped out onto the patio. Immediately, and spontaneously, people stood to greet her, clapping and smiling. Mabel responded by throwing kisses. A flock of Canada Geese—in perfect V formation—flew over the site, like air force planes. It was an unexpected salute.

Charlene and Rich led her to her seat in the front.

Grace was seated at a keyboard and as soon as they were settled, she began an introduction and Rochelle stood up to sing. Many of the guests wouldn't recognize the song but it brought back lots of memories for the older ones and was Mabel's favorite.

"Because you come to me with naught save love,

And hold my hand and lift mine eyes above ..."

The words went straight to Mabel's heart. She had wanted a sacred, quiet wedding,

"Because God made thee mine, I'll cherish thee

Through light and darkness ..."

As soon as the song was over, Noah stepped out of Etta's apartment door, followed by Tucker and Ed. Charlene and her mother joined them below the trellis.

"Dearly beloved, we are gathered together here in the sight of God to join this man and this woman in holy matrimony." Noah's voice was steady and confident.

Tucker stood on her right, his strong frame giving her support. They exchanged rings and almost, it seemed to Mabel, before it started, Noah said, "And now, I pronounce you man and wife."

Tucker bent his head down and kissed her just as Gevano began to sing, "The Lord's Prayer."

They remained still, heads bowed as Gevano sang:

"Our Father, who art in heaven, Hallowed be Thy name,

Thy kingdom come, Thy will be done on earth

As it is in heaven."

"Now you may kiss your bride," Noah announced, smiling, and Tucker kissed her again.

Mabel and Tucker turned to face the guests and were mobbed first by their grandchildren. Sue and Charlene finally moved them aside and the bride and groom started down the aisle to greet guests. Mabel hung on to Tucker because walking on thick grass was a huge challenge to her.

At the far end of Bougainvillea Hall, Charlene, Sue and Tucker's daughter, Jeanne had set up a beautiful table with refreshments and a four-tier wedding cake. Mabel wondered if they had planned for this crowd! Tucker was greeted more like a King than a groom, and he looked like royalty in his navy suit and blue-green tie. He was thanking people for bringing their potted plants and flowers for decorations.

Cutting the cake seemed to take longer than the marriage ceremony, but eventually the bride and groom were able to slip away to change into casual clothes. When they came down from the apartment to leave, a crowd of friends cheered them and Barry leaned over to open the front door of the Mabel's fully decorated Honda.

Tucker took a few steps in their direction, exclaiming about the signs on Mabel's car. "Do you really believe that people would look at these, then at Mabel and me and believe we were just married?"

Ed drove up in his gray Buick and Tucker helped his bride into the front seat, and hurried around to take Ed's place. They looked back at the opened mouths and heard yells of frustration. "Enjoy Disney World," Ryan called, holding up the brochure from the front seat of the Honda.

"And I hope you enjoy washing Mabel's car!" Tucker responded.

Tucker laughed all the way to the Interstate, then he took Mabel's hand and pressed it against his cheek. "You are beautiful, Mrs. Quick."

"The wedding was absolutely superb, Tucker. How did you manage all the chairs and the flowers?"

"I rented the chairs and I asked people to bring their

potted plants and flowers. They loved doing it."

"You just know how to ask people to do things!" Mabel said proudly.

"Like asking a certain woman to marry me?"

"You did a lot better job of that than I did." They both laughed. It was a shared, private moment that belonged to just the two of them. Mabel grew serious. "I thought I had ruined any chances with you, Tucker."

"Mrs. Quick, you can do anything you want to do, but you cannot get rid of me. … It says so on my wedding band."

"Oh, it doesn't!" Mabel said and took hers off. She admired it for a moment.

"It says you belong to me until death do we part."

"The jeweler did a wonderful job and put our names on the rings just as Willie drew them. Your name is nestled within mine. Is that okay with you, dear wife?"

"Everything is okay with me, dear husband." She leaned against him and he began to hum "Because."

They both tried to sing it but the words wouldn't come to them, so they just laughed, held hands and traveled down the road on their honeymoon.

A New Beginning …

About the author:

Lila and Richard Hopkins have lived in a Continuing Care Retirement Community for nearly nine years. Lila dreaded the move from their beloved mountain home to Fuquay Varina, N. C. but soon fell in love with the residents and staff at Windsor Point. The move, and heart surgery at Duke Medical Center, probably saved Richard's life, so it was well worth it. The Hopkins will soon celebrate 62 years of marriage.

Lila had written for her church denomination for years before she retired from teaching and wrote her first novel—a children's book, ***Eating Crow.*** That book and its sequel, ***Talking Turkey***, won the North Carolina Juvenile Literature Award.

She began writing regional novels after Richard retired from the ministry and they moved to Linville, N.C. Ingalls Publishing Group published, ***Weave Me A Song, Strike a Golden Chord,*** and ***The Master Craftsman.*** Each book won the Book of The Year award from High Country Writers.

The Hopkins have four children and seven grandchildren. Their daughter and one son live in N.C. and two other sons live in California, in the Bay Area.

Lila continues to teach—a Memoir Writing Class at Windsor Point.

Made in the USA
Charleston, SC
28 April 2012